BABYMOUSE AND FRIENDS*

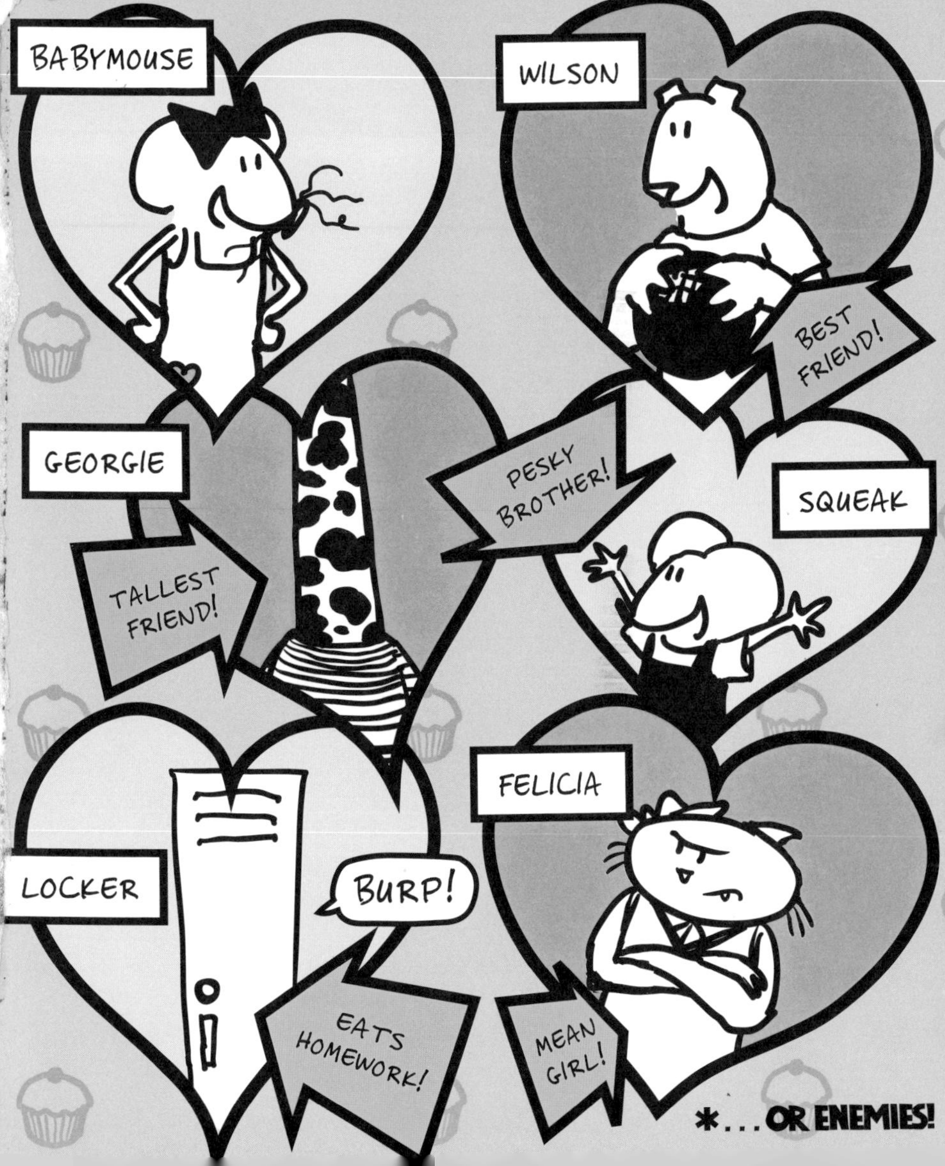
BABYMOUSE
WILSON
BEST FRIEND!
GEORGIE
TALLEST FRIEND!
PESKY BROTHER!
SQUEAK
LOCKER
BURP!
EATS HOMEWORK!
FELICIA
MEAN GIRL!

*. . . OR ENEMIES!

NO ONE CAN READ JUST ONE!

Be sure to read **ALL** the **BABYMOUSE** books:

#1 BABYMOUSE: Queen of the World!
#2 BABYMOUSE: Our Hero
#3 BABYMOUSE: Beach Babe
#4 BABYMOUSE: Rock Star
#5 BABYMOUSE: Heartbreaker
#6 CAMP BABYMOUSE
#7 BABYMOUSE: Skater Girl
#8 BABYMOUSE: Puppy Love
#9 BABYMOUSE: Monster Mash
#10 BABYMOUSE: The Musical
#11 BABYMOUSE: Dragonslayer
#12 BABYMOUSE: Burns Rubber
#13 BABYMOUSE: Cupcake Tycoon
#14 BABYMOUSE: Mad Scientist
#15 A Very BABYMOUSE Christmas
#16 BABYMOUSE for President
#17 Extreme BABYMOUSE
#18 Happy Birthday, BABYMOUSE

BABYMOUSE
QUEEN OF THE WORLD!

BY JENNIFER L. HOLM & MATTHEW HOLM

RANDOM HOUSE NEW YORK

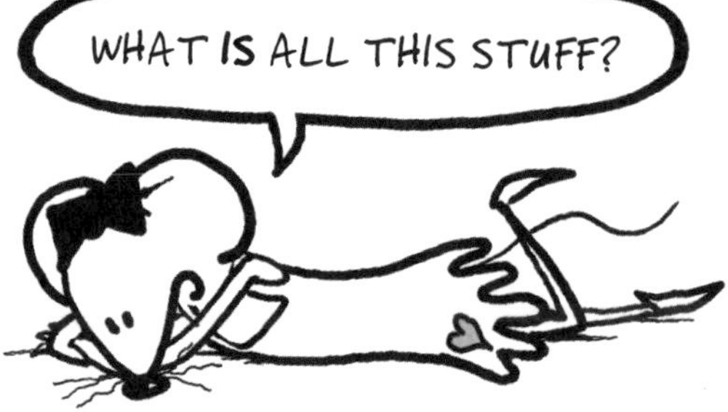
WHAT IS ALL THIS STUFF?

 Published in the United States by Random House Children's Books, a division of Random House, Inc., New York.

Random House and the colophon are registered trademarks of Random House, Inc.

Visit us on the Web!
randomhouse.com/kids
Babymouse.com

Educators and librarians, for a variety of teaching tools, visit us at
RHTeachersLibrarians.com

Library of Congress Cataloging-in-Publication Data
Holm, Jennifer L.
Babymouse : queen of the world! / Jennifer Holm and Matthew Holm
p. cm.
Summary: An imaginative mouse dreams of being queen of the world, but will settle for an invitation to the most popular girl's slumber party.
ISBN 978-0-375-83229-1 (trade) — ISBN 978-0-375-93229-8 (lib. bdg.)
[1. Popularity—Fiction. 2. Imagination—Fiction. 3. Friendship—Fiction.
4. Mice—Fiction. 5. Animals—Fiction. 6. Cartoons and comics.]
I. Holm, Matthew. II. Title.
PN6727.H592B33 2005 741.5'973—dc22 2004051166

MANUFACTURED IN MALAYSIA 25 24 23 22 21 20 19 18 17 16 15 14

Random House Children's Books supports the First Amendment and celebrates the right to read.

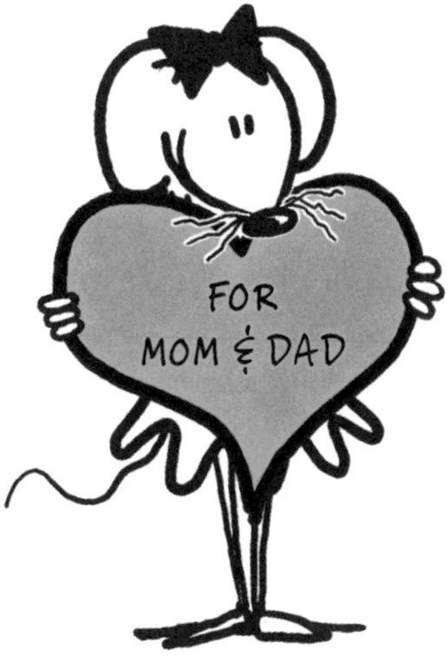
FOR
MOM & DAD

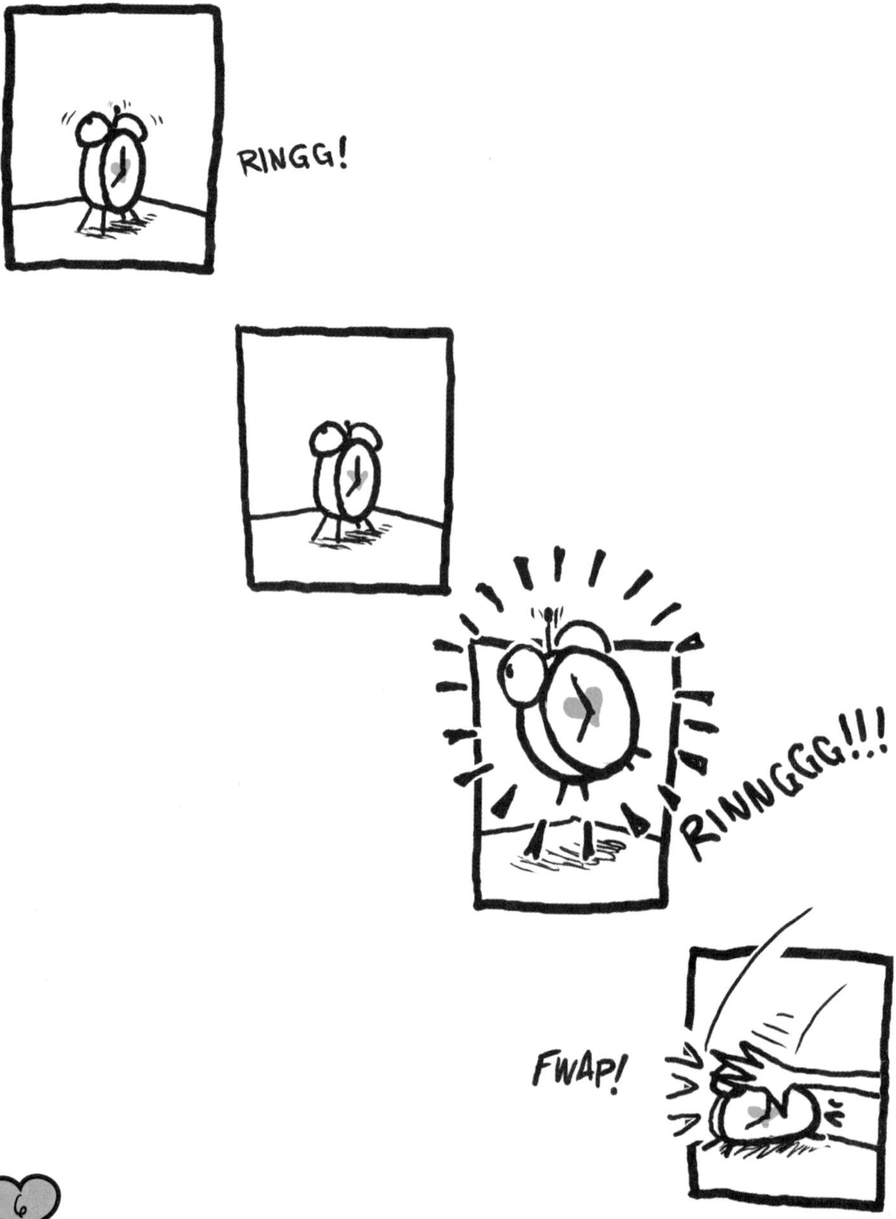
RINGG!
RINNGGG!!!
FWAP!

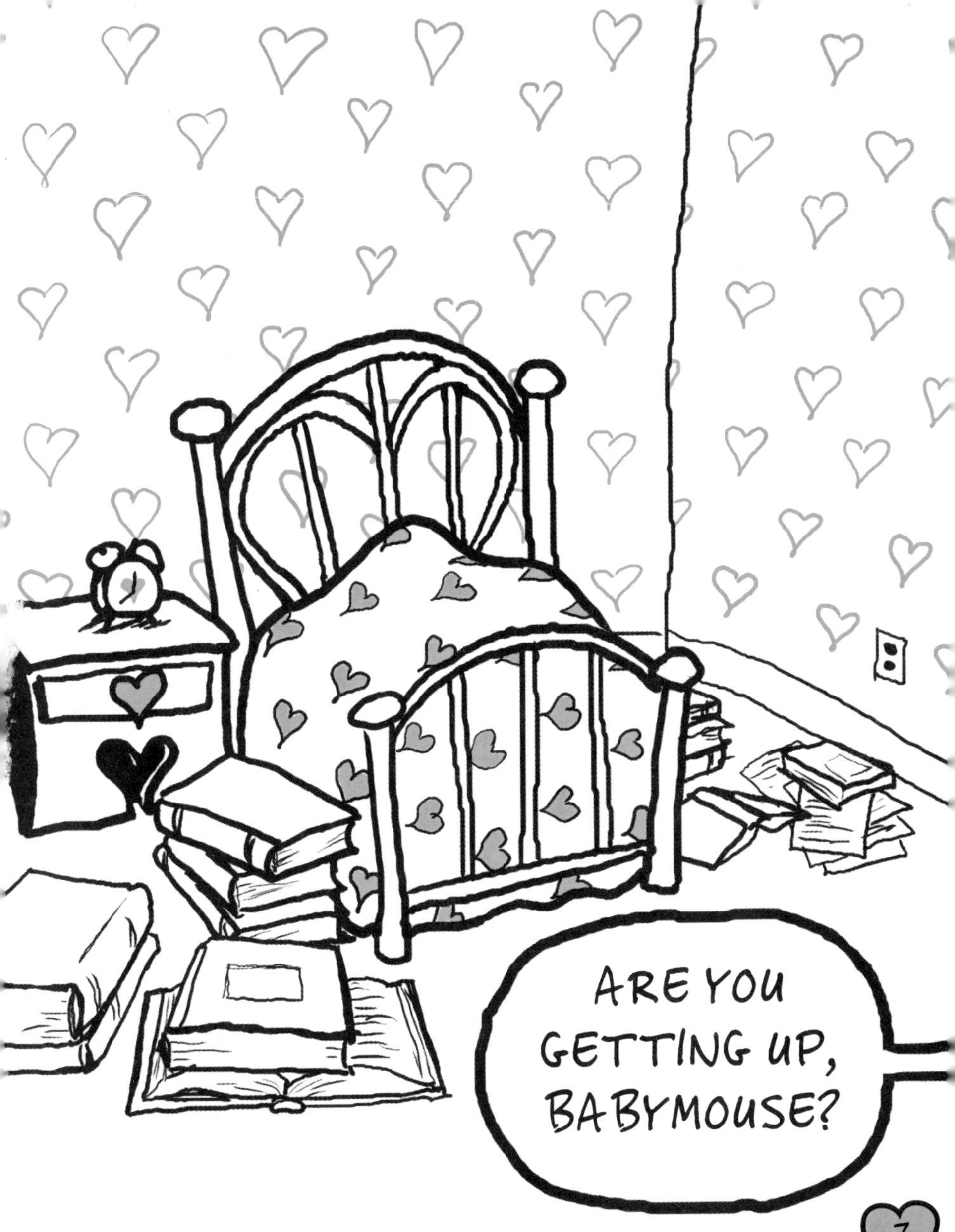
ARE YOU GETTING UP, BABYMOUSE?

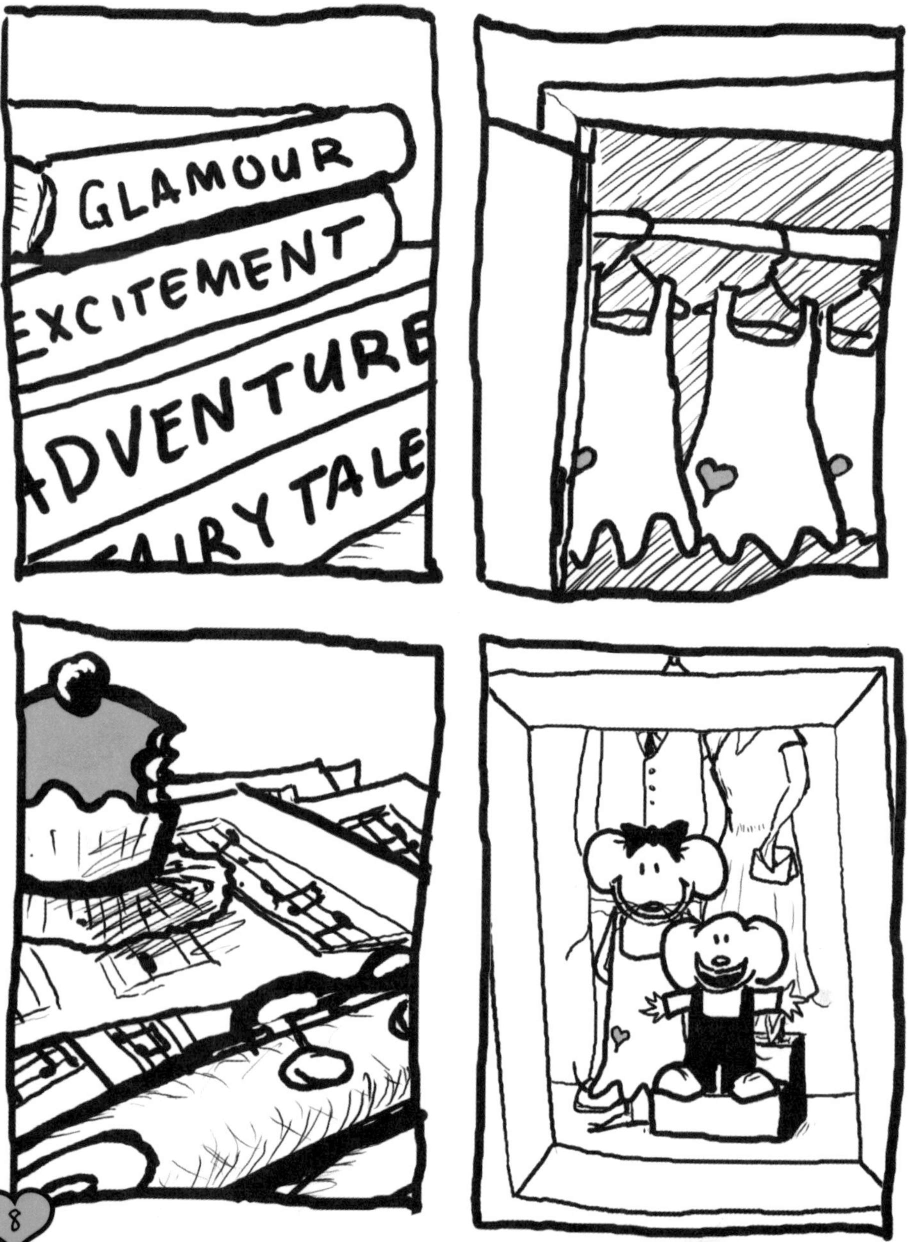
GLAMOUR
EXCITEMENT
DVENTURE
AIRY TALE

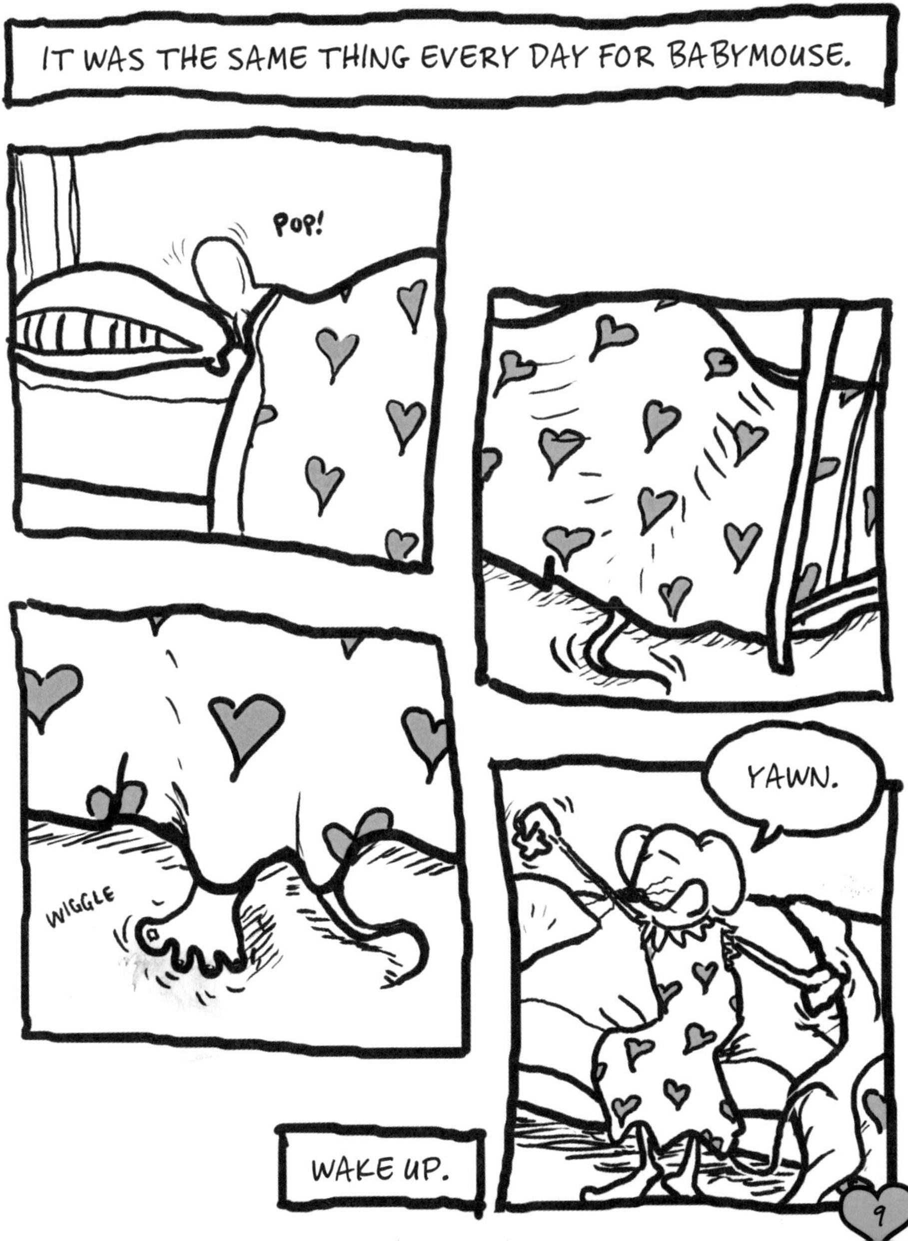
IT WAS THE SAME THING EVERY DAY FOR BABYMOUSE.
POP!
WIGGLE
YAWN.
WAKE UP.

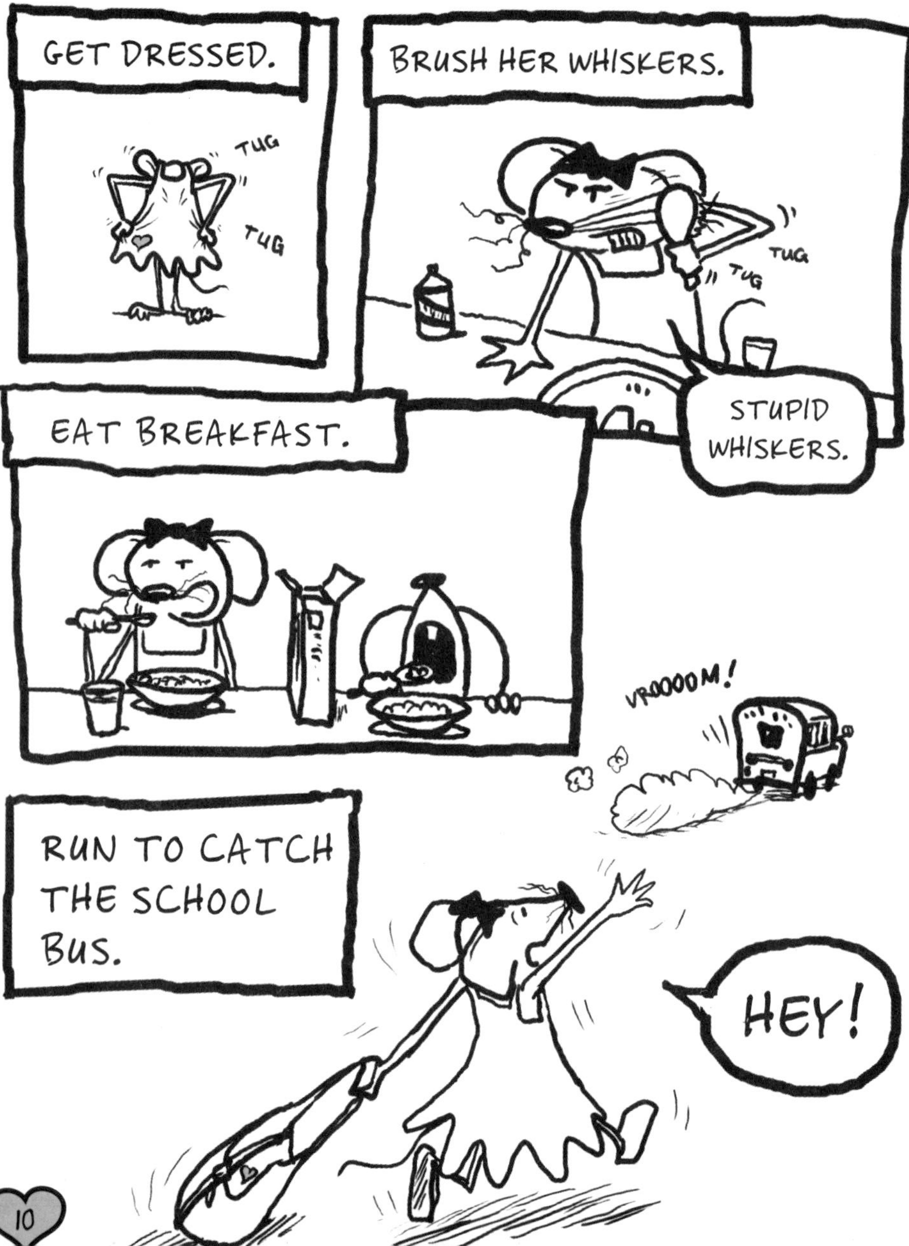
GET DRESSED.
TUG
TUG
BRUSH HER WHISKERS.
TUG
TUG
STUPID WHISKERS.
EAT BREAKFAST.
VROOOOM!
RUN TO CATCH THE SCHOOL BUS.
HEY!

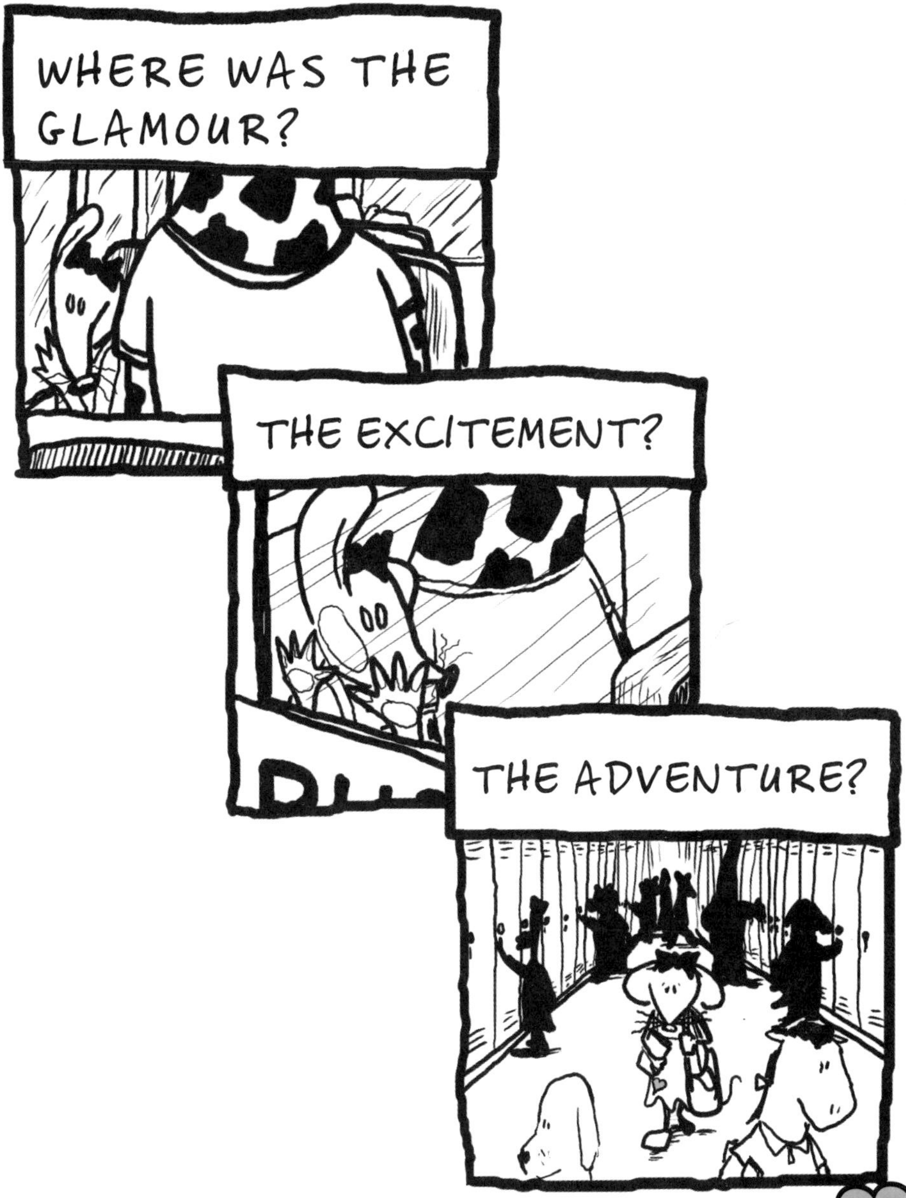

WHERE WAS THE GLAMOUR?
THE EXCITEMENT?
THE ADVENTURE?

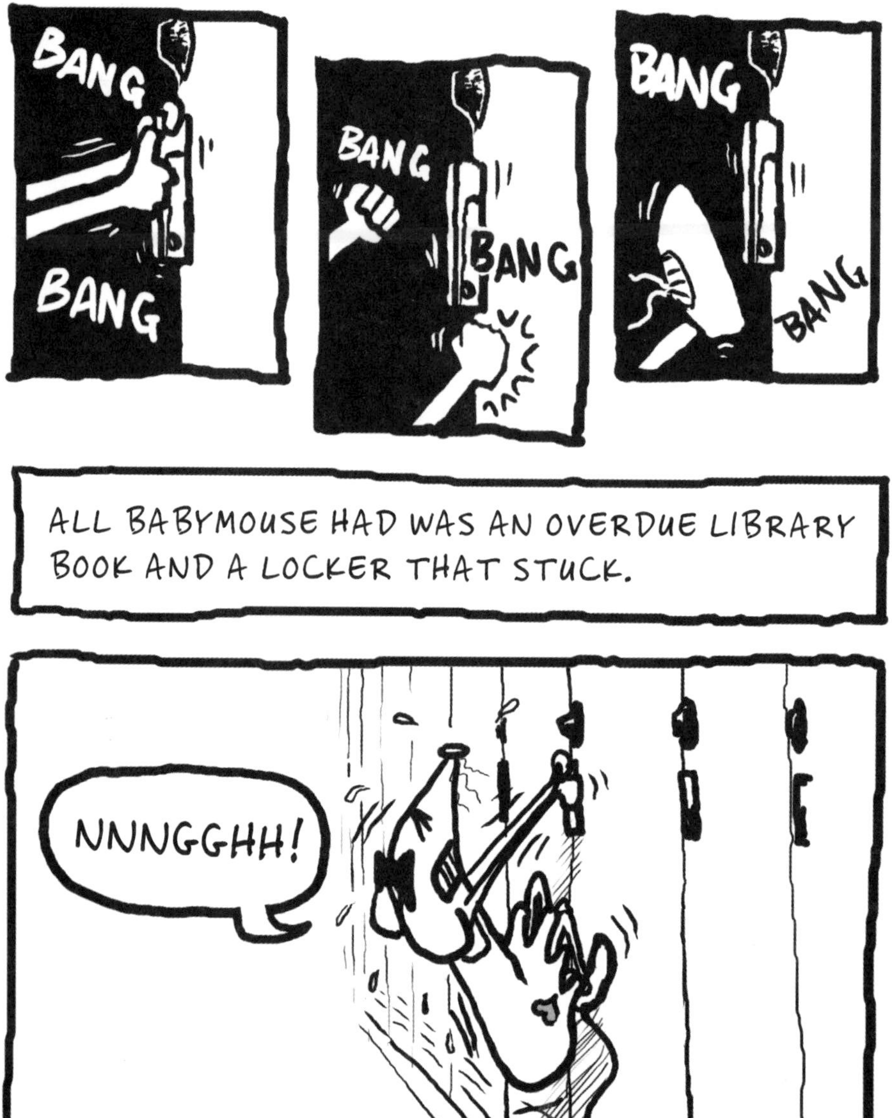
BANG
BANG
BANG
BANG
BANG
BANG
ALL BABYMOUSE HAD WAS AN OVERDUE LIBRARY BOOK AND A LOCKER THAT STUCK.
NNNGGHH!

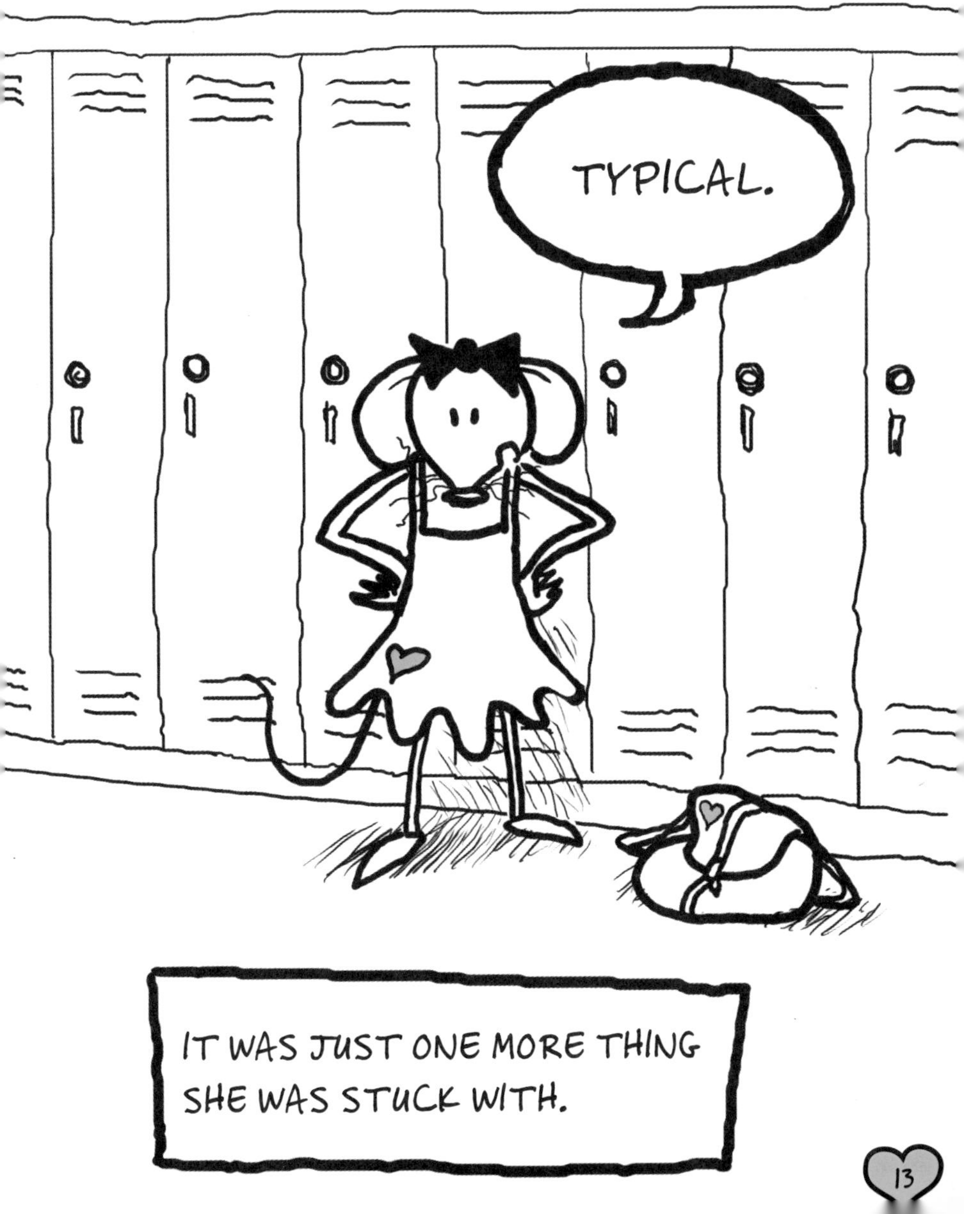
TYPICAL.

IT WAS JUST ONE MORE THING SHE WAS STUCK WITH.

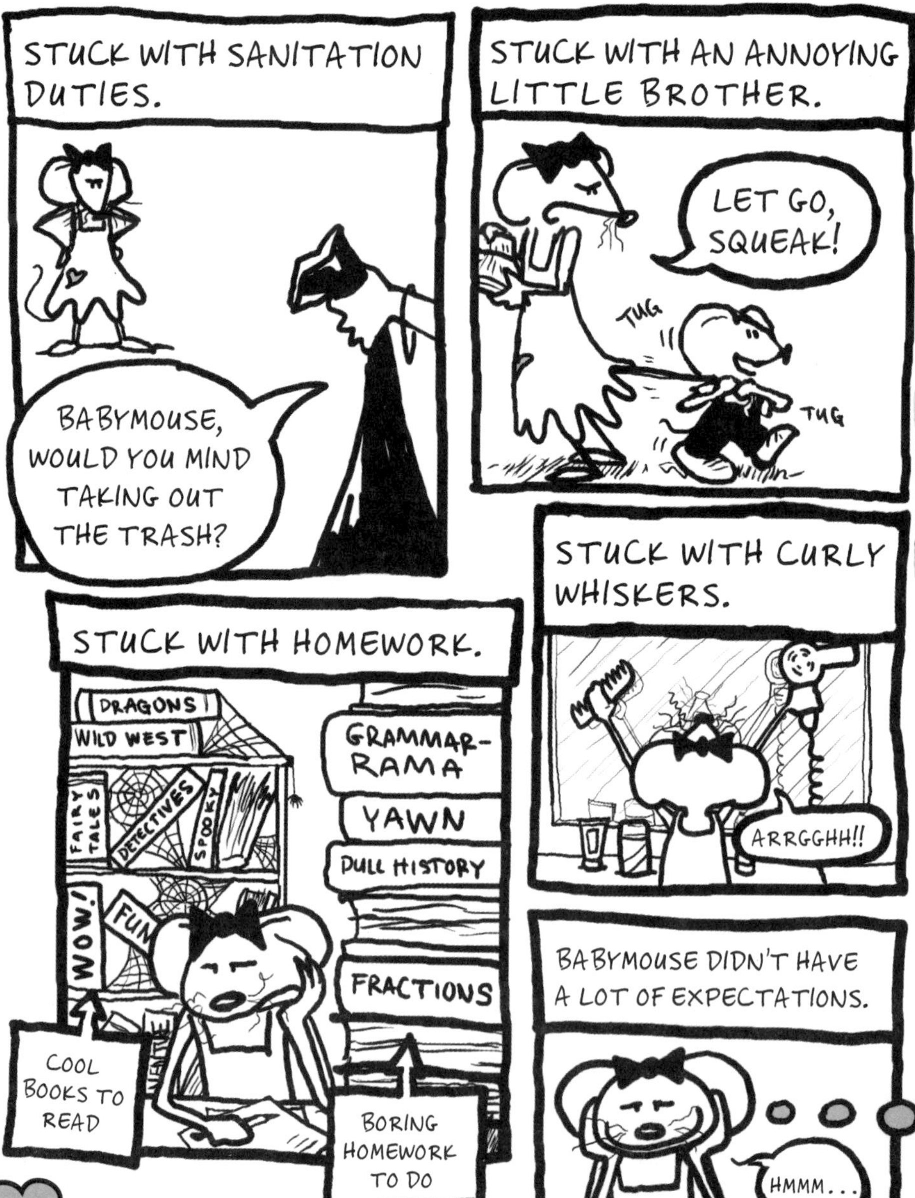
STUCK WITH SANITATION DUTIES.
BABYMOUSE, WOULD YOU MIND TAKING OUT THE TRASH?
STUCK WITH AN ANNOYING LITTLE BROTHER.
LET GO, SQUEAK!
TUG
TUG
STUCK WITH CURLY WHISKERS.
ARRGGHH!!
STUCK WITH HOMEWORK.
DRAGONS
WILD WEST
FAIRY TALES
DETECTIVES
SPOOKY
WOW!
FUN
GRAMMAR-RAMA
YAWN
DULL HISTORY
FRACTIONS
COOL BOOKS TO READ
BORING HOMEWORK TO DO
BABYMOUSE DIDN'T HAVE A LOT OF EXPECTATIONS.
HMMM...

WELL, MAYBE JUST A FEW.
TIARA!
ICE CREAM FOR LUNCH!
STRAIGHT WHISKERS!
NO HOMEWORK!
QUEEN OF THE WORLD!

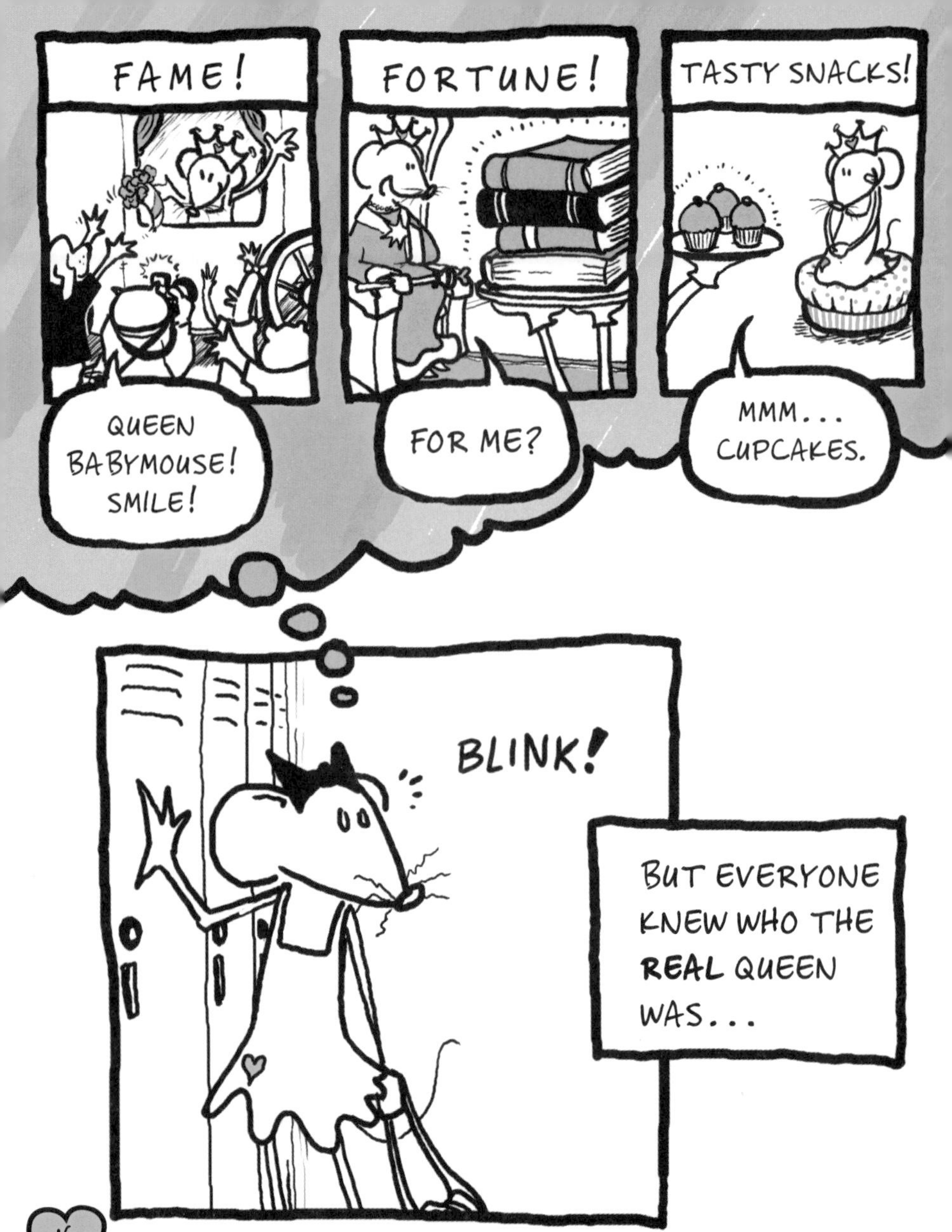
FAME!
QUEEN BABYMOUSE! SMILE!
FORTUNE!
FOR ME?
TASTY SNACKS!
MMM... CUPCAKES.
BLINK!
BUT EVERYONE KNEW WHO THE **REAL** QUEEN WAS...

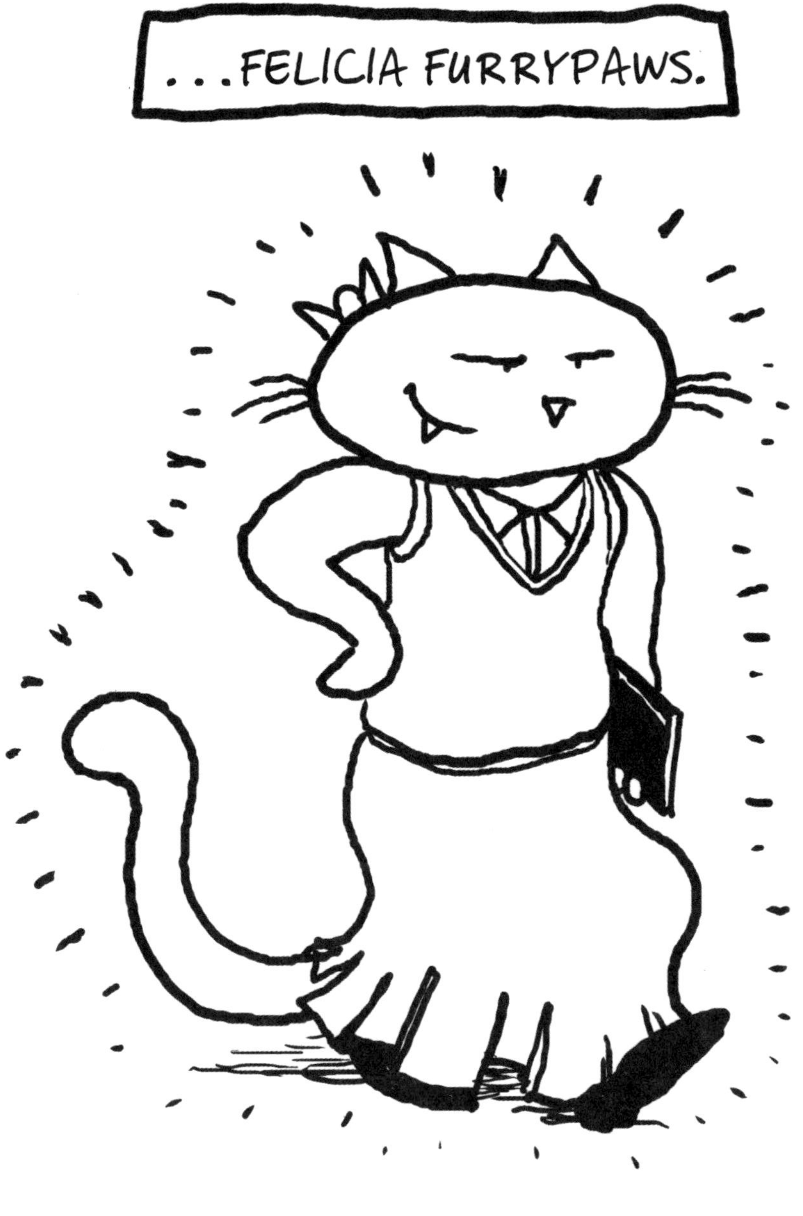
...FELICIA FURRYPAWS.

I FOR LUNCH TODAY. ISN'T THAT
'S BETTER THAN THAT MEAT
E. YUCK! I WONDER IF IT EVEN HAS
NALLY, I DON'T REALLY LIKE ANY
RD "LOAF" IN IT. WELL, EXCEPT
COUNT? I GUESS NOT. OH—AND
HE NEATEST BOOK, ABOUT THIS
A WIZARD AND GETS TO GO TO
OL. ISN'T THAT COOL? I WISH WE
OL. THEN WE COULD LEARN TO DO
STUFF INSTEAD OF HAVING TO LE
CTIONS. FELICIA,
OKAY... BE COOL...

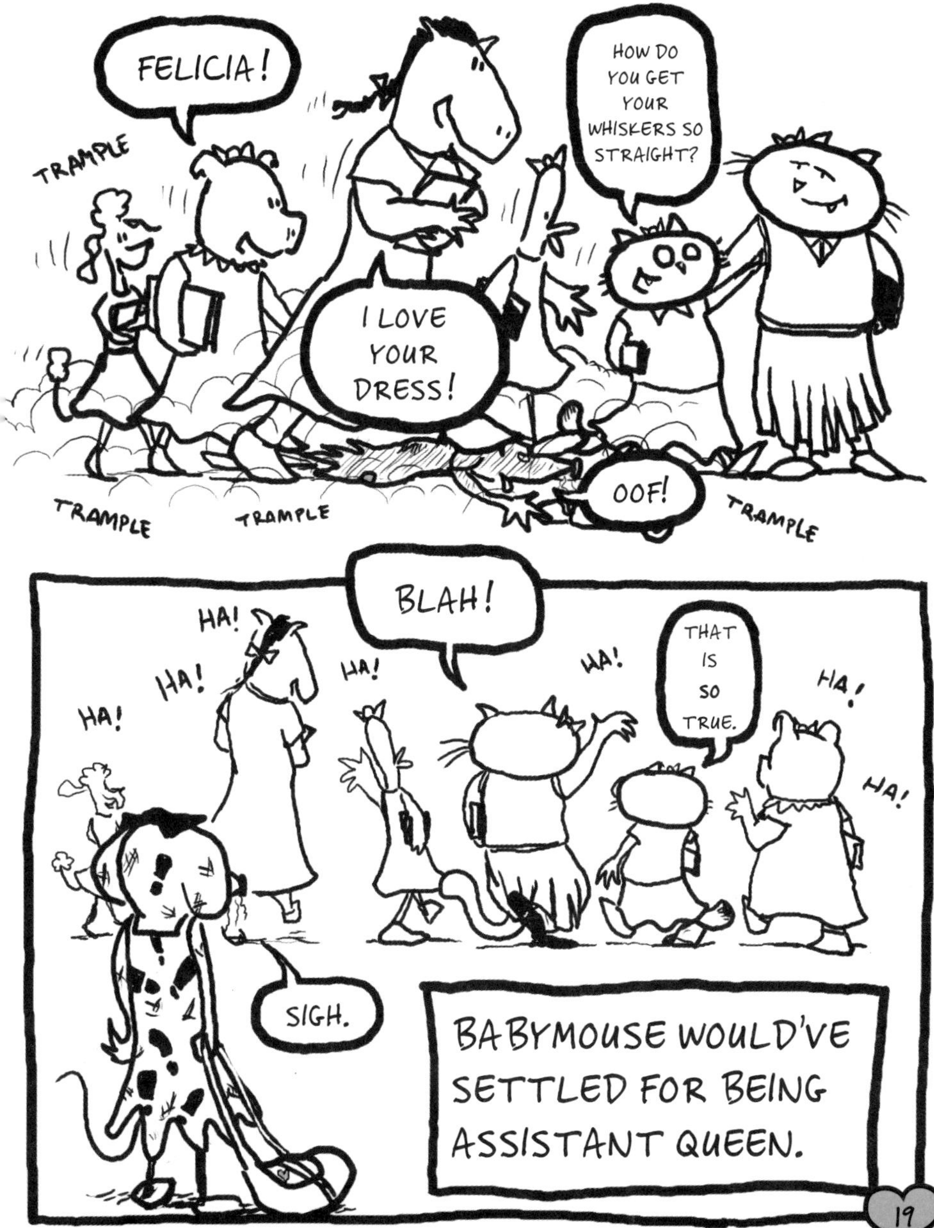

FELICIA!
TRAMPLE
HOW DO YOU GET YOUR WHISKERS SO STRAIGHT?
I LOVE YOUR DRESS!
TRAMPLE
TRAMPLE
OOF!
TRAMPLE
BLAH!
HA!
HA!
HA!
HA!
HA!
THAT IS SO TRUE.
HA!
HA!
SIGH.
BABYMOUSE WOULD'VE SETTLED FOR BEING ASSISTANT QUEEN.

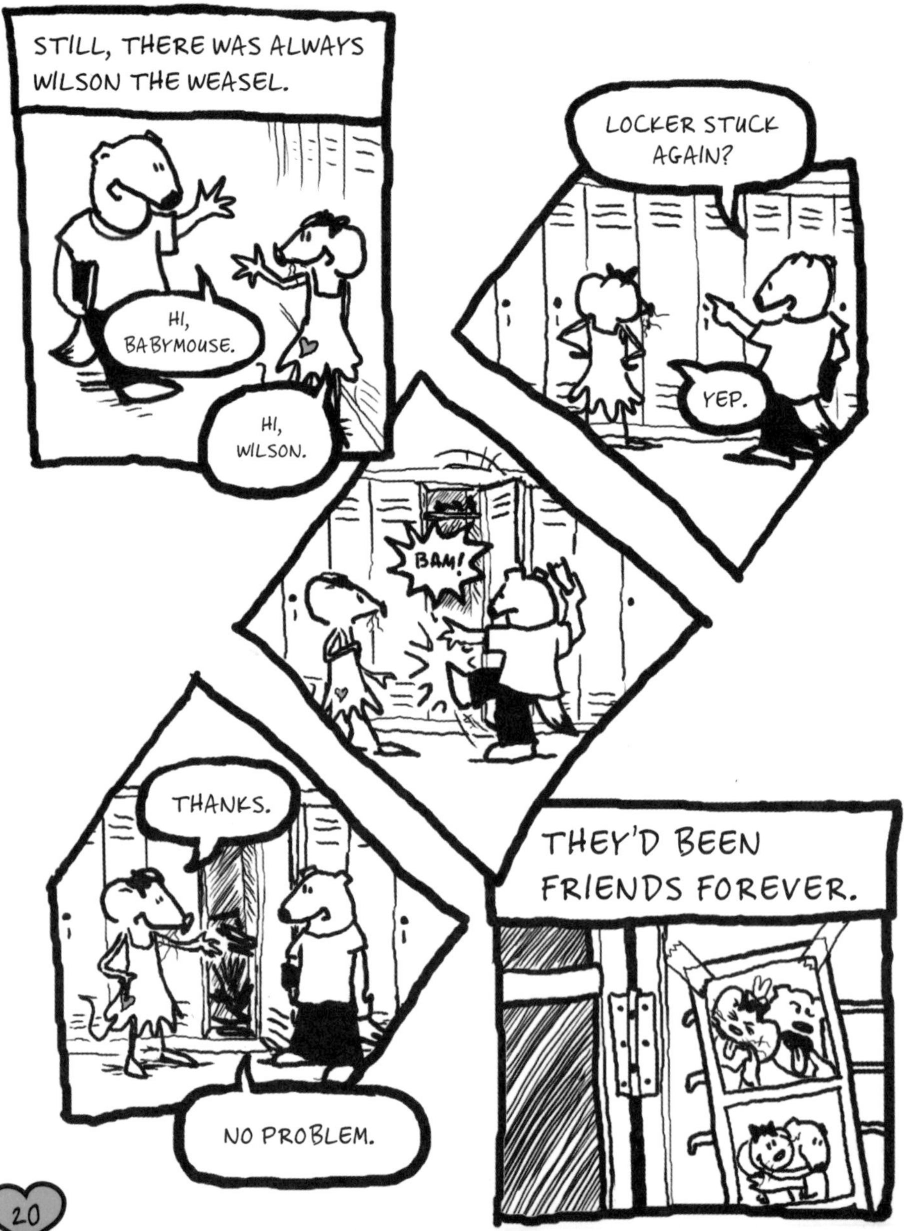

STILL, THERE WAS ALWAYS WILSON THE WEASEL.
HI, BABYMOUSE.
HI, WILSON.
LOCKER STUCK AGAIN?
YEP.
BAM!
THANKS.
NO PROBLEM.
THEY'D BEEN FRIENDS FOREVER.

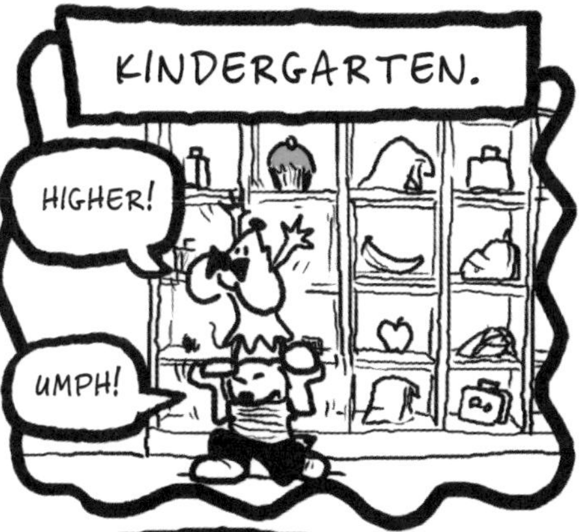
KINDERGARTEN.
HIGHER!
UMPH!

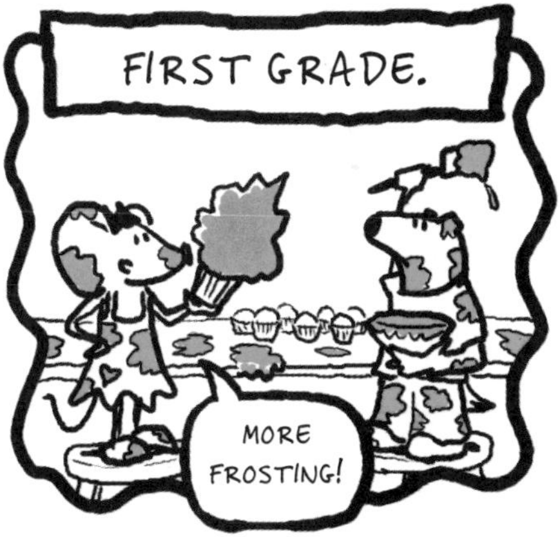
FIRST GRADE.
MORE FROSTING!

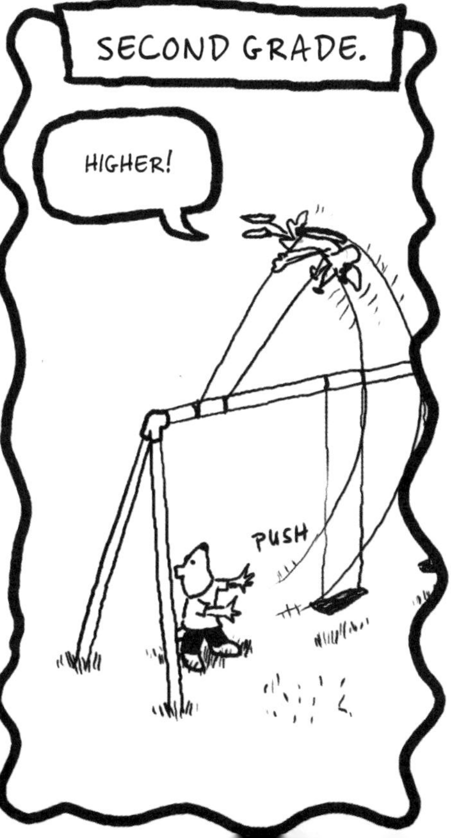
SECOND GRADE.
HIGHER!
PUSH

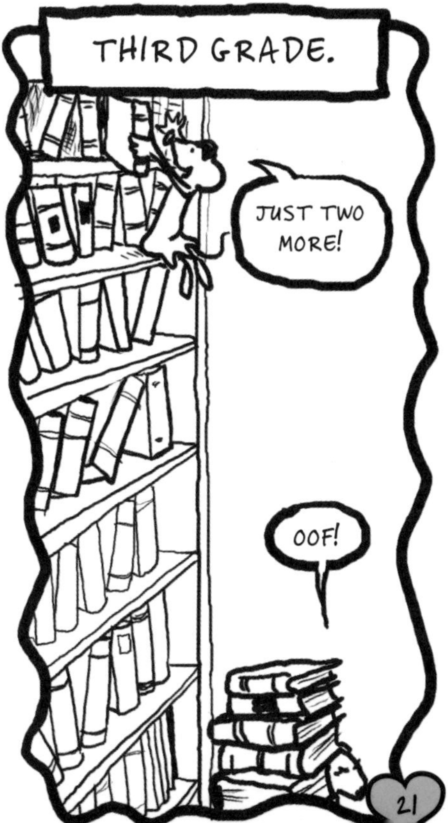
THIRD GRADE.
JUST TWO MORE!
OOF!

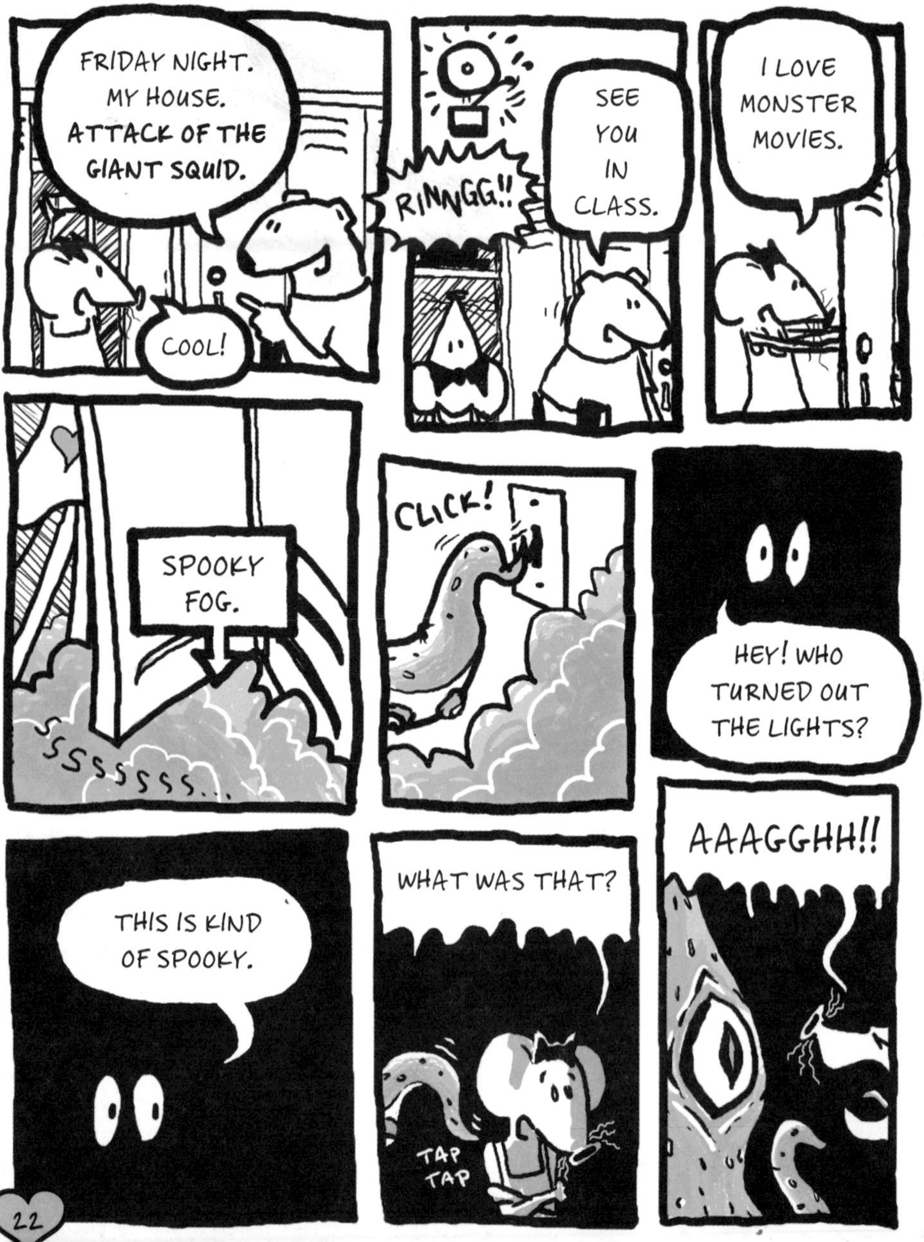
FRIDAY NIGHT. MY HOUSE. ATTACK OF THE GIANT SQUID.
COOL!
RINNGG!!
SEE YOU IN CLASS.
I LOVE MONSTER MOVIES.
SPOOKY FOG.
SSSSSSSS...
CLICK!
HEY! WHO TURNED OUT THE LIGHTS?
THIS IS KIND OF SPOOKY.
WHAT WAS THAT?
TAP TAP
AAAGGHH!!

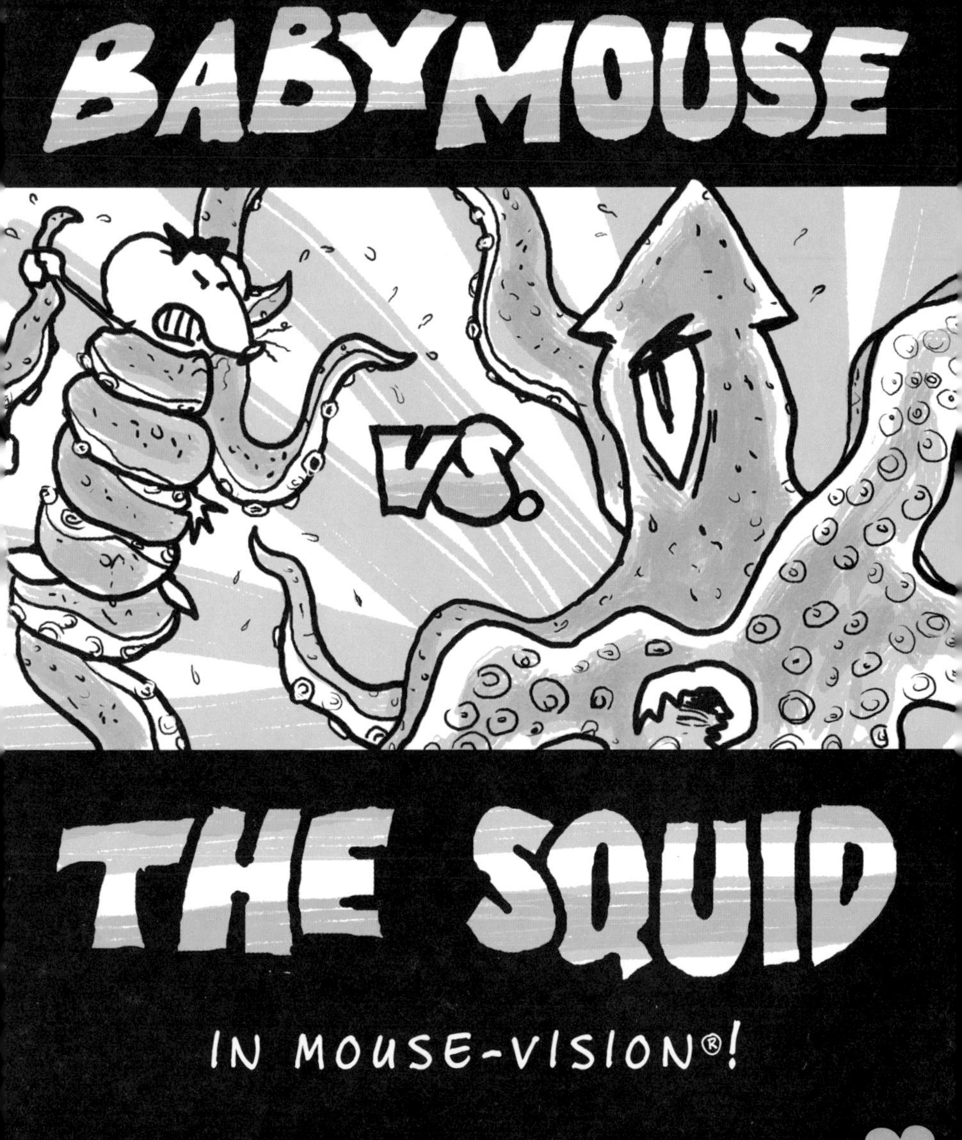
BABYMOUSE
VS.
THE SQUID
IN MOUSE-VISION®!

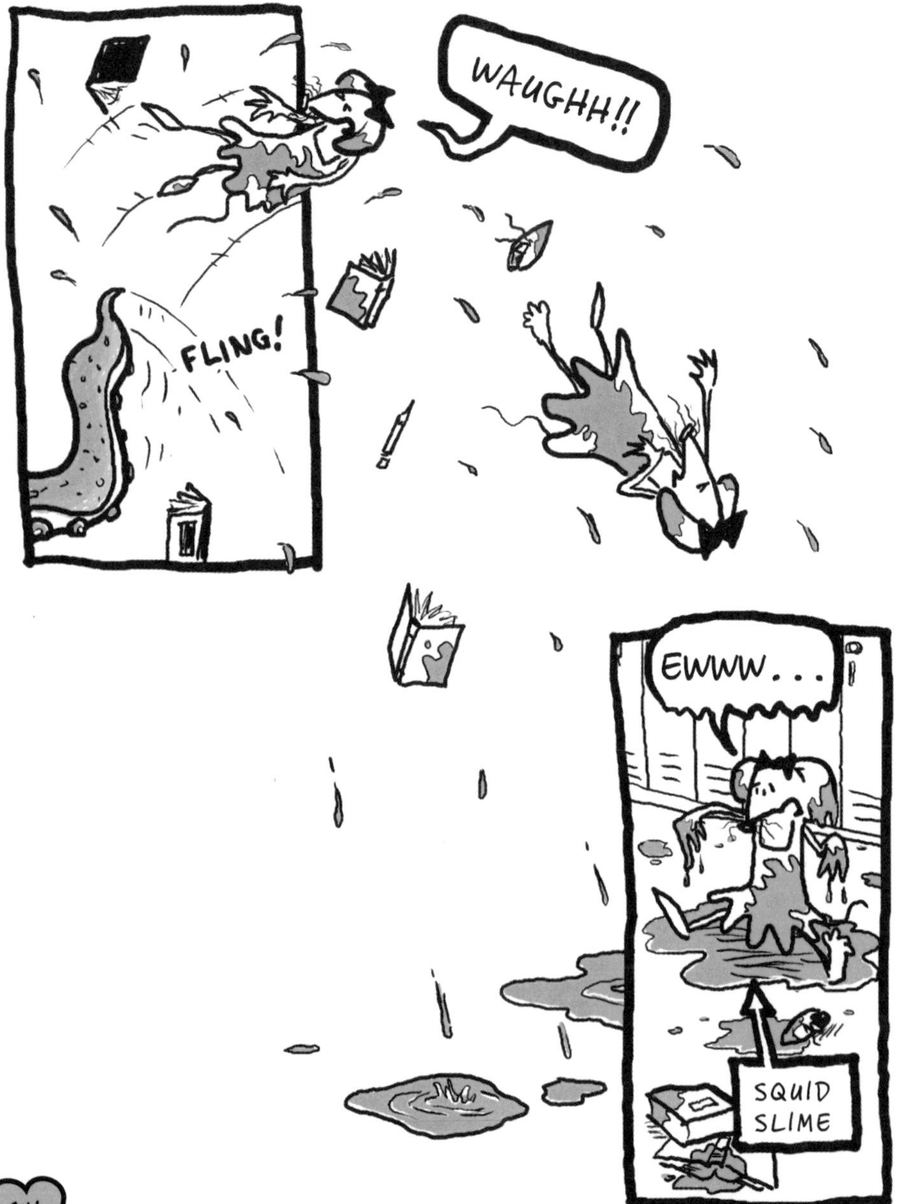
FLING!
WAUGHH!!
EWWW...
SQUID SLIME

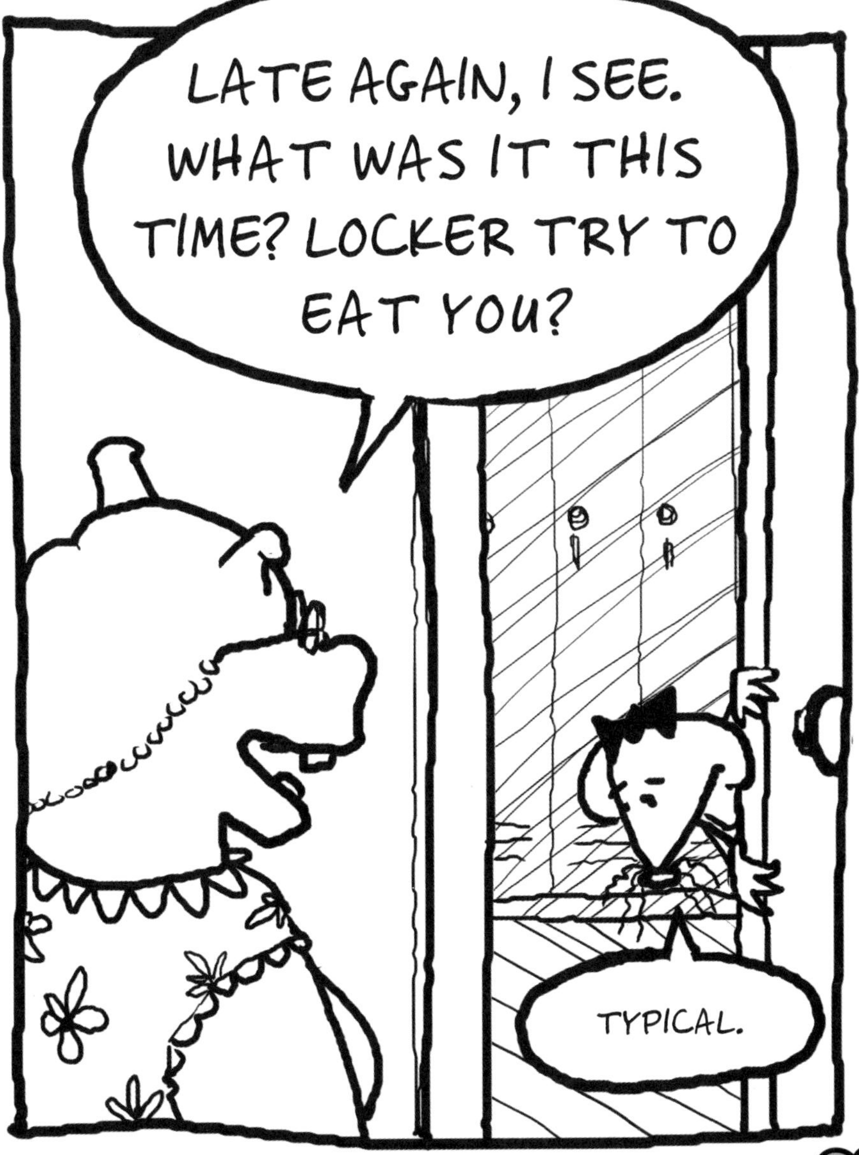
LATE AGAIN, I SEE. WHAT WAS IT THIS TIME? LOCKER TRY TO EAT YOU?
TYPICAL.

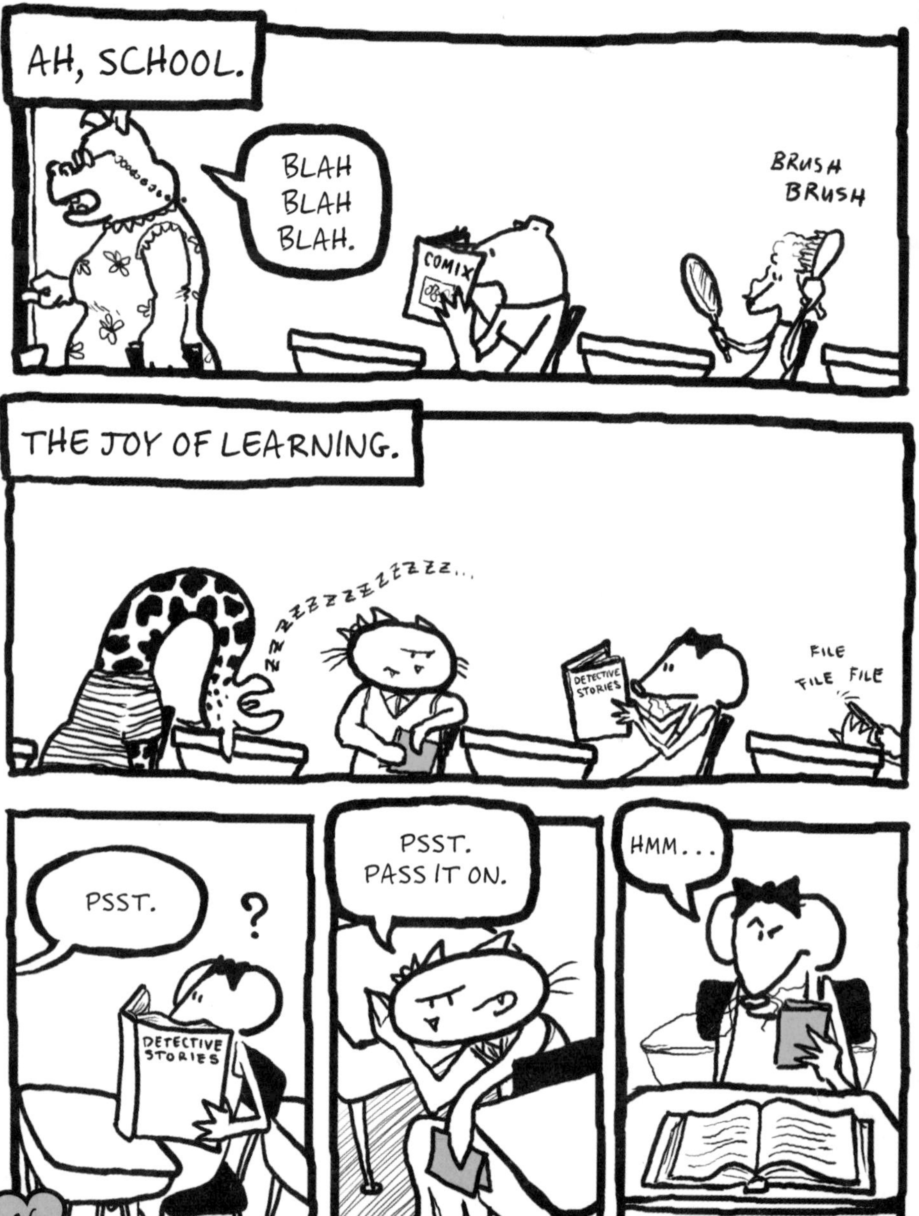

AH, SCHOOL.
BLAH BLAH BLAH.
COMIX
BRUSH BRUSH
THE JOY OF LEARNING.
ZZZZZZZZZZZZZZZ...
DETECTIVE STORIES
FILE FILE FILE
PSST.
?
DETECTIVE STORIES
PSST. PASS IT ON.
HMM...

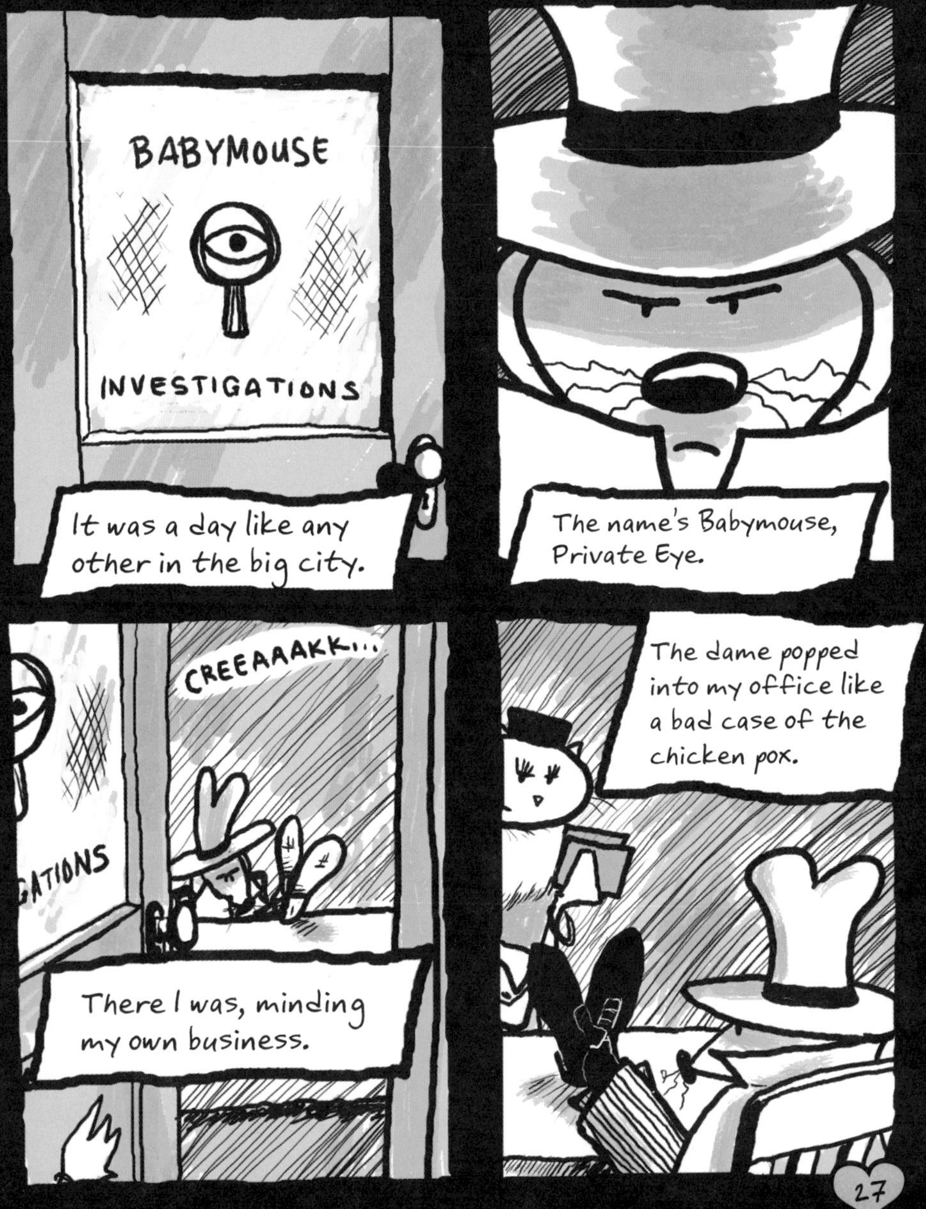
BABYMOUSE
INVESTIGATIONS
It was a day like any other in the big city.
The name's Babymouse, Private Eye.
CREEAAAKK...
GATIONS
There I was, minding my own business.
The dame popped into my office like a bad case of the chicken pox.

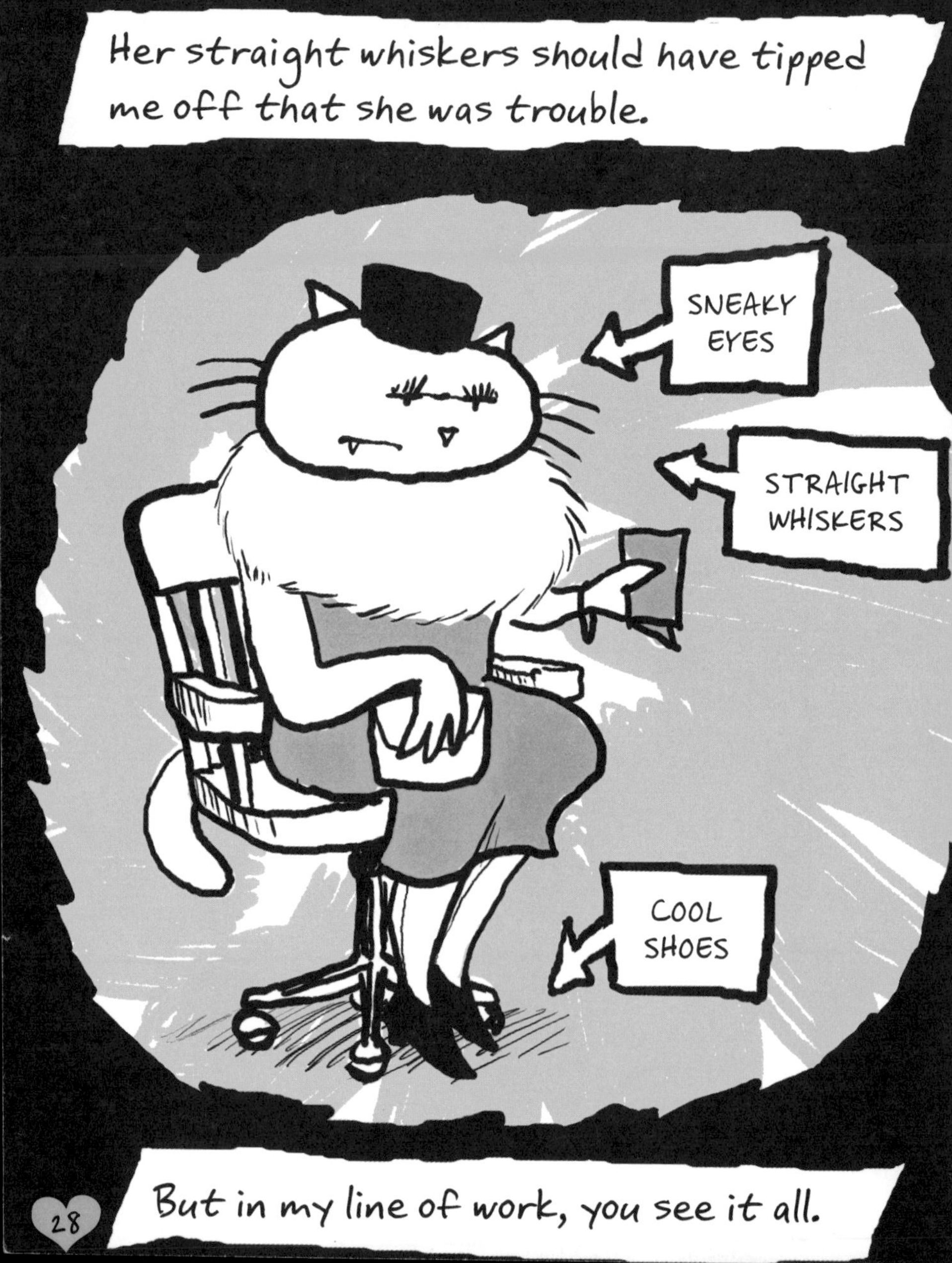
Her straight whiskers should have tipped me off that she was trouble.
SNEAKY EYES
STRAIGHT WHISKERS
COOL SHOES
But in my line of work, you see it all.

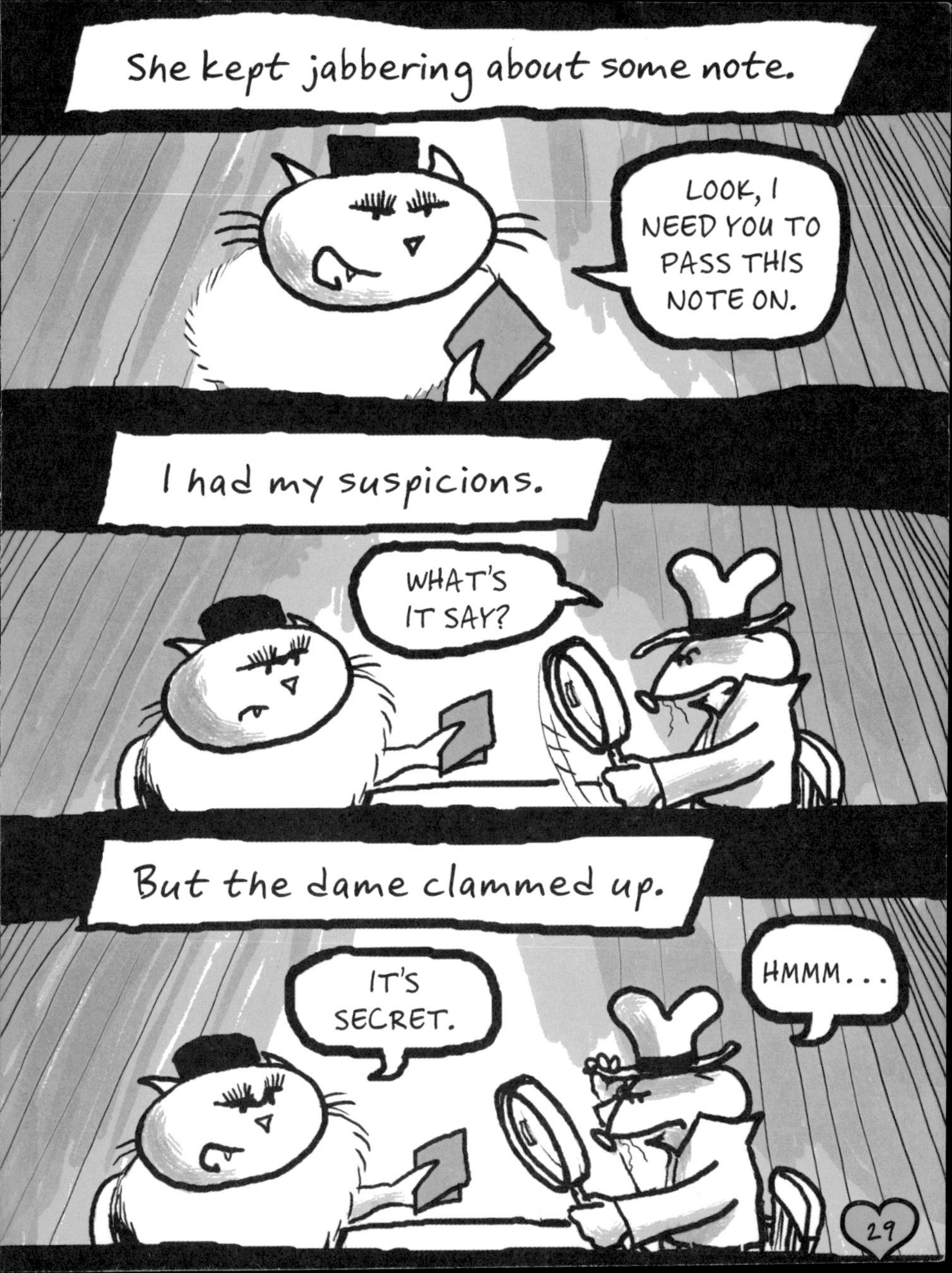
She kept jabbering about some note.
LOOK, I NEED YOU TO PASS THIS NOTE ON.
I had my suspicions.
WHAT'S IT SAY?
But the dame clammed up.
IT'S SECRET.
HMMM...

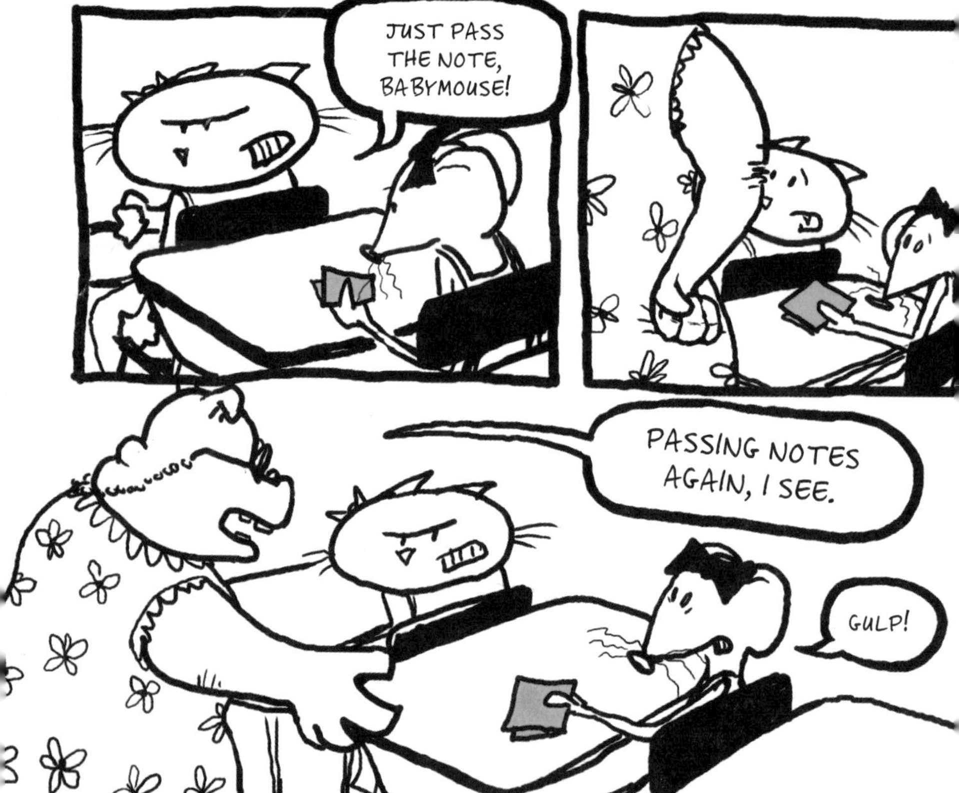
JUST PASS THE NOTE, BABYMOUSE!
PASSING NOTES AGAIN, I SEE.
GULP!
WAY TO GO, BABYMOUSE.
PRINC
OFFI
MAYBE YOU SHOULD GIVE UP DETECTIVE WORK, BABYMOUSE.
SIGH.

LUNCHTIME...WHERE THE FOOD WAS DEFINITELY NOT FIT FOR A QUEEN— OR EVEN AN ASSISTANT QUEEN.

EWW.

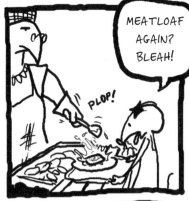

MEATLOAF AGAIN? BLEAH!

PLOP!

NOT TO MENTION, SOMEONE WAS SITTING ON BABYMOUSE'S THRONE.

THERE'S NO ROOM, BABYMOUSE.

TYPICAL.

WHERE'S A PRINCE WHEN YOU NEED HIM, ANYWAY?

OVER HERE, BABYMOUSE! I SAVED YOU A SEAT.

31

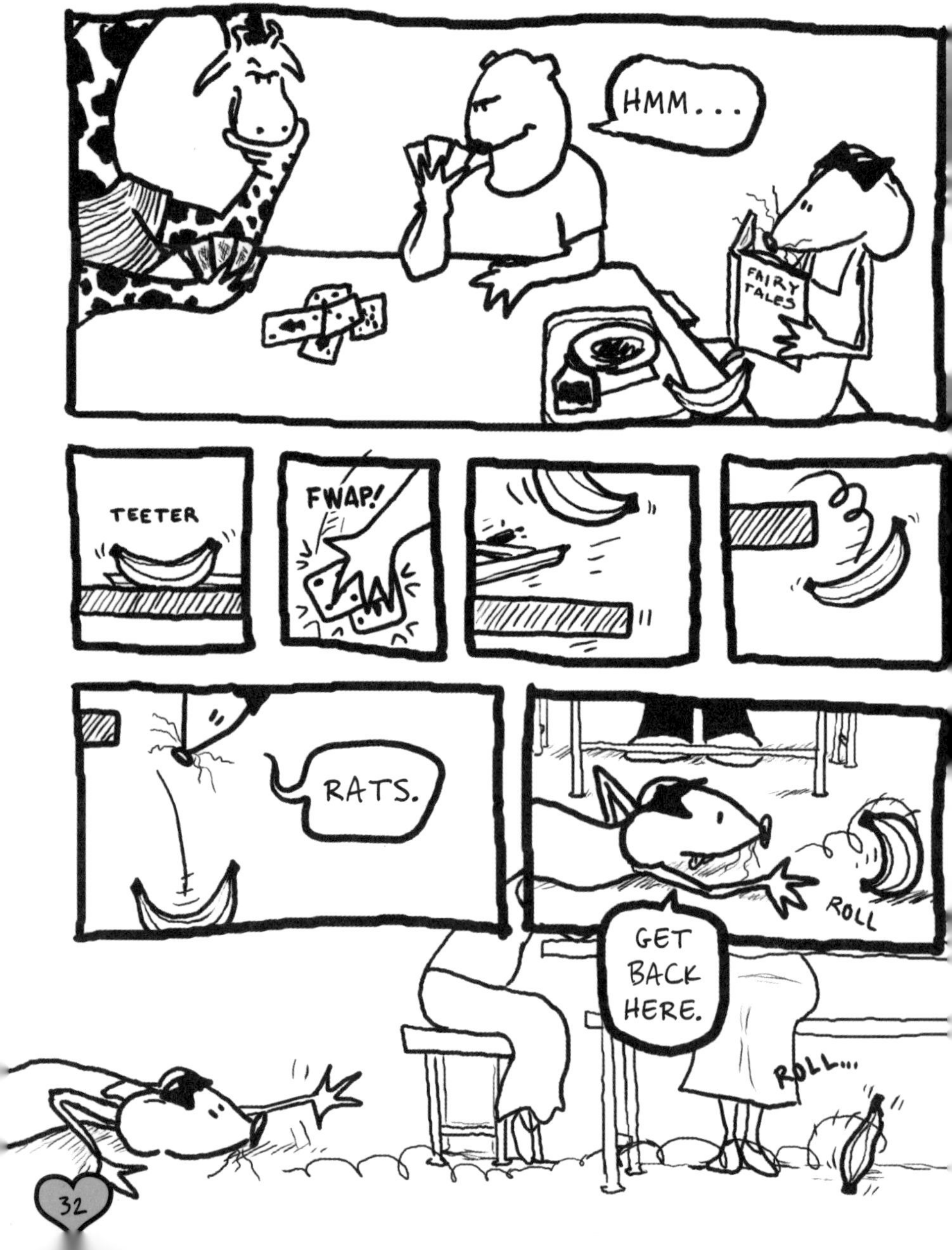
HMM...
FAIRY TALES
TEETER
FWAP!
RATS.
ROLL
GET BACK HERE.
ROLL...

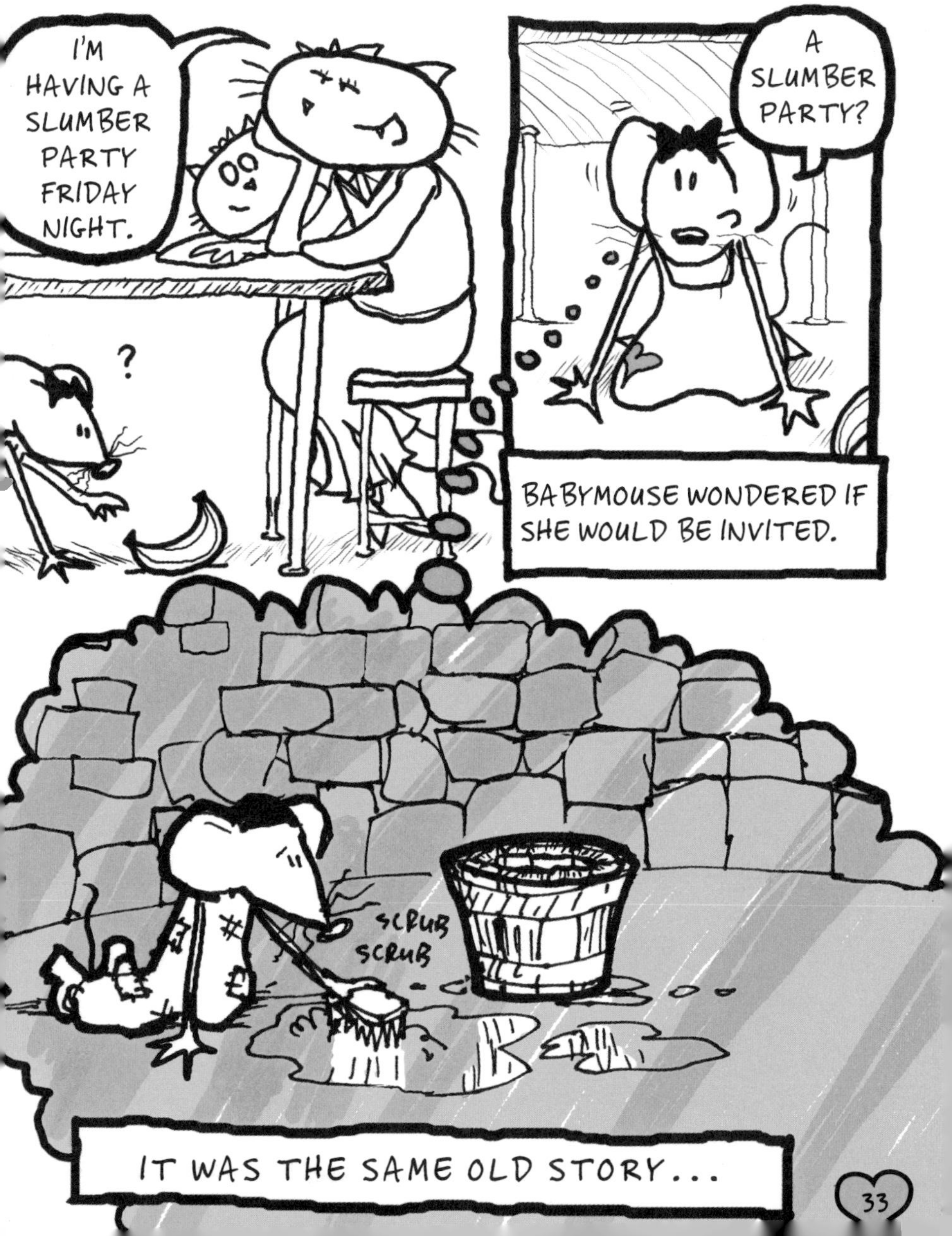
I'M HAVING A SLUMBER PARTY FRIDAY NIGHT.
A SLUMBER PARTY?
BABYMOUSE WONDERED IF SHE WOULD BE INVITED.
SCRUB SCRUB
IT WAS THE SAME OLD STORY . . .

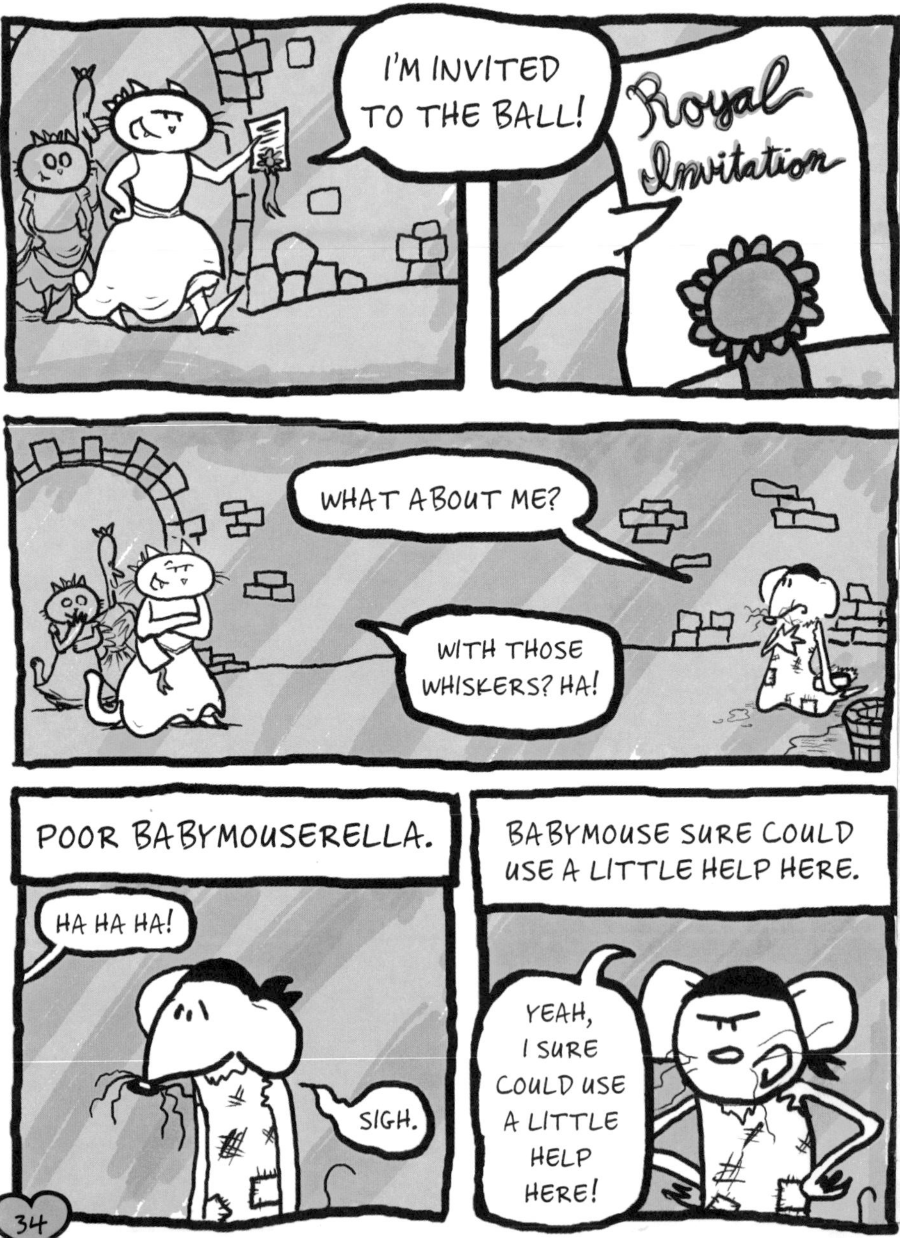
I'M INVITED TO THE BALL!
Royal Invitation
WHAT ABOUT ME?
WITH THOSE WHISKERS? HA!
POOR BABYMOUSERELLA.
HA HA HA!
SIGH.
BABYMOUSE SURE COULD USE A LITTLE HELP HERE.
YEAH, I SURE COULD USE A LITTLE HELP HERE!

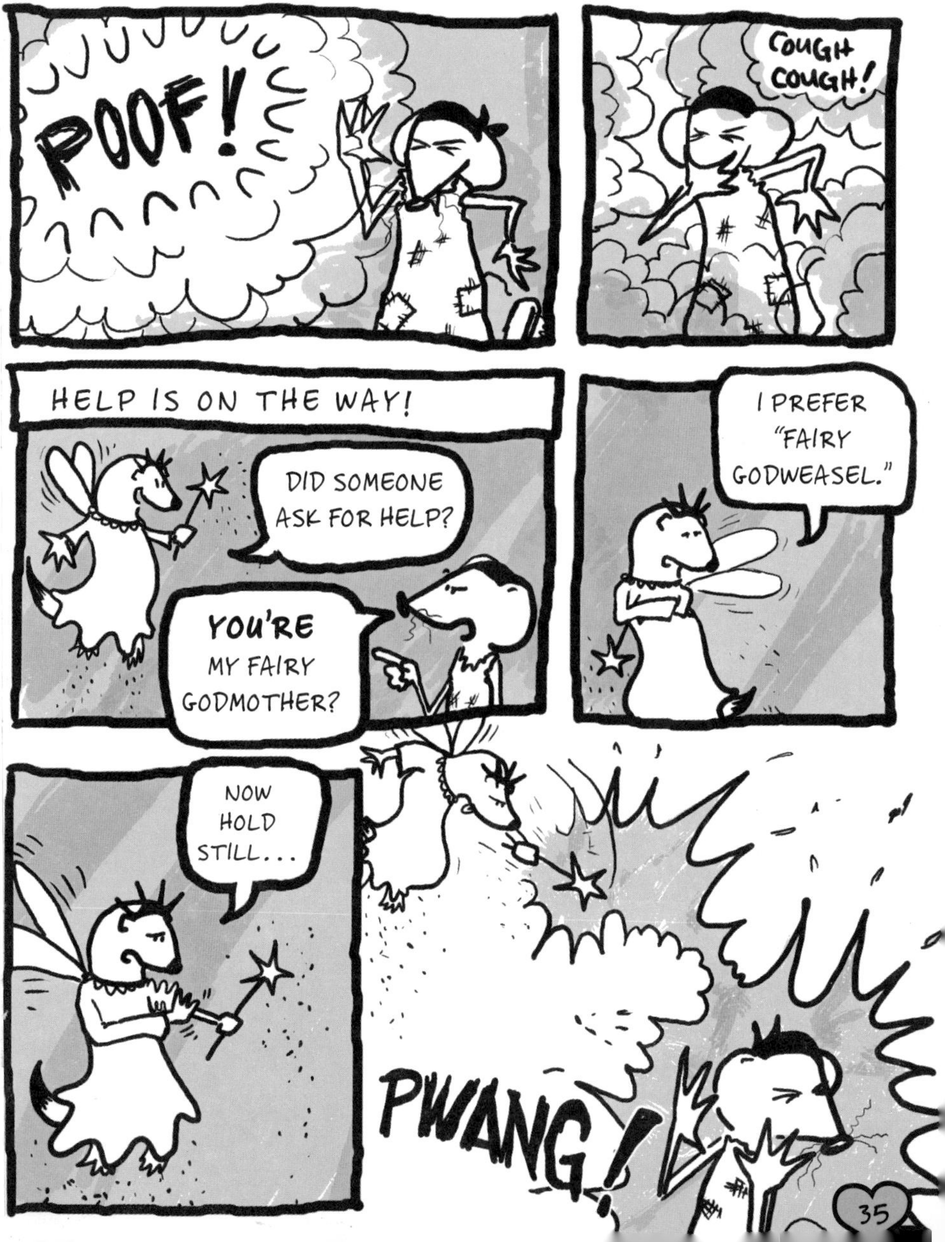
POOF!
COUGH COUGH!
HELP IS ON THE WAY!
DID SOMEONE ASK FOR HELP?
YOU'RE MY FAIRY GODMOTHER?
I PREFER "FAIRY GODWEASEL."
NOW HOLD STILL...
PWANG!

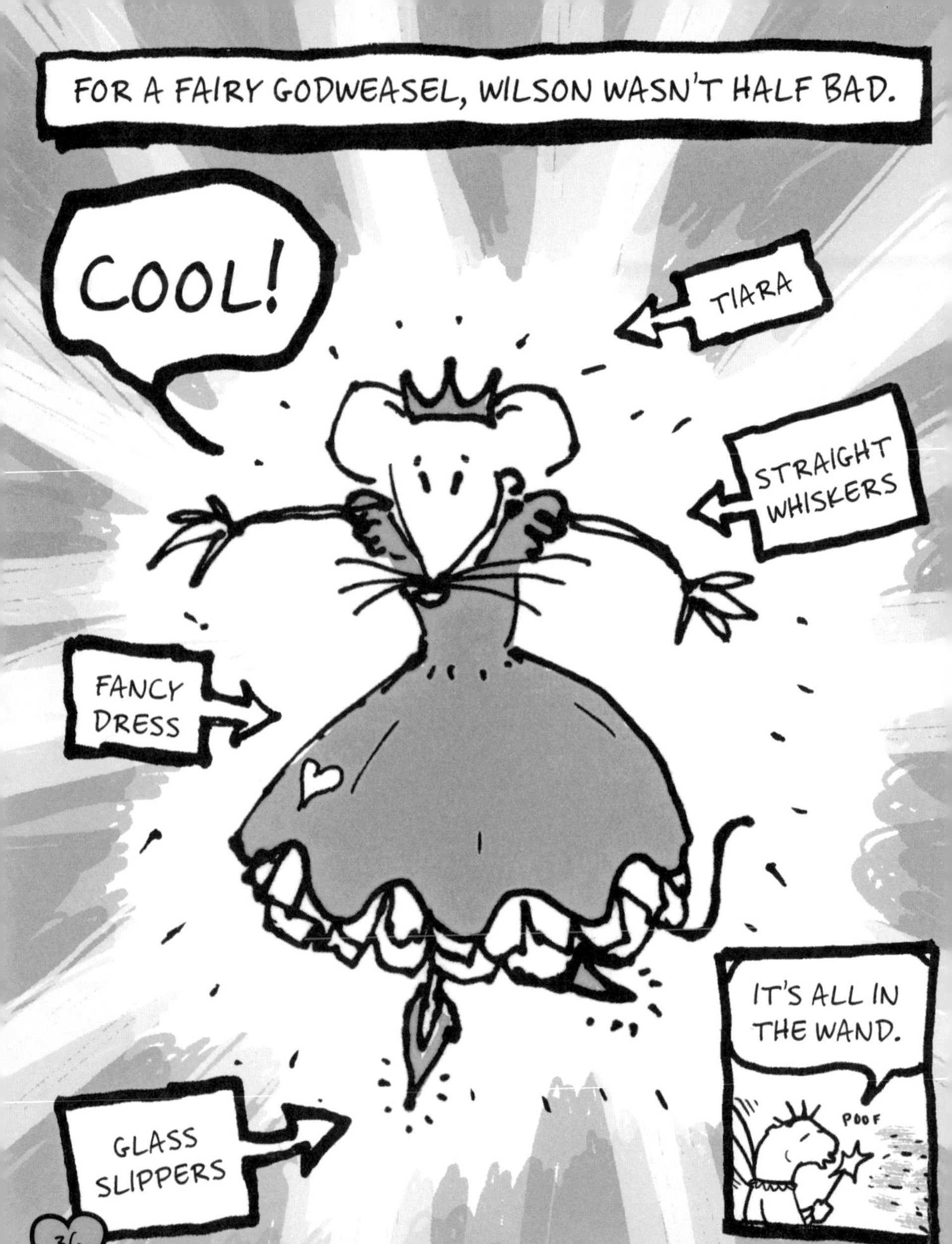
FOR A FAIRY GODWEASEL, WILSON WASN'T HALF BAD.
COOL!
TIARA
STRAIGHT WHISKERS
FANCY DRESS
GLASS SLIPPERS
IT'S ALL IN THE WAND.
POOF

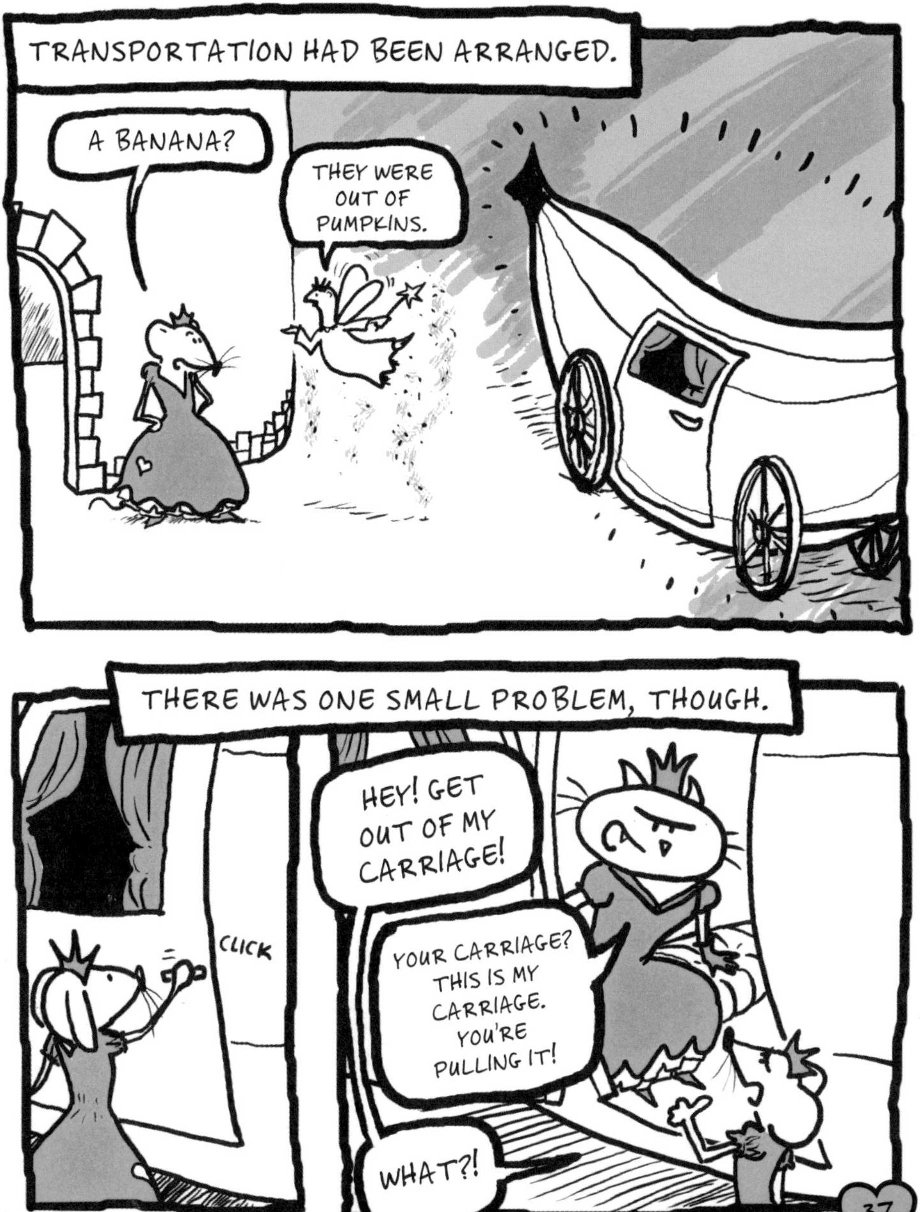
TRANSPORTATION HAD BEEN ARRANGED.
A BANANA?
THEY WERE OUT OF PUMPKINS.
THERE WAS ONE SMALL PROBLEM, THOUGH.
CLICK
HEY! GET OUT OF MY CARRIAGE!
YOUR CARRIAGE? THIS IS MY CARRIAGE. YOU'RE PULLING IT!
WHAT?!

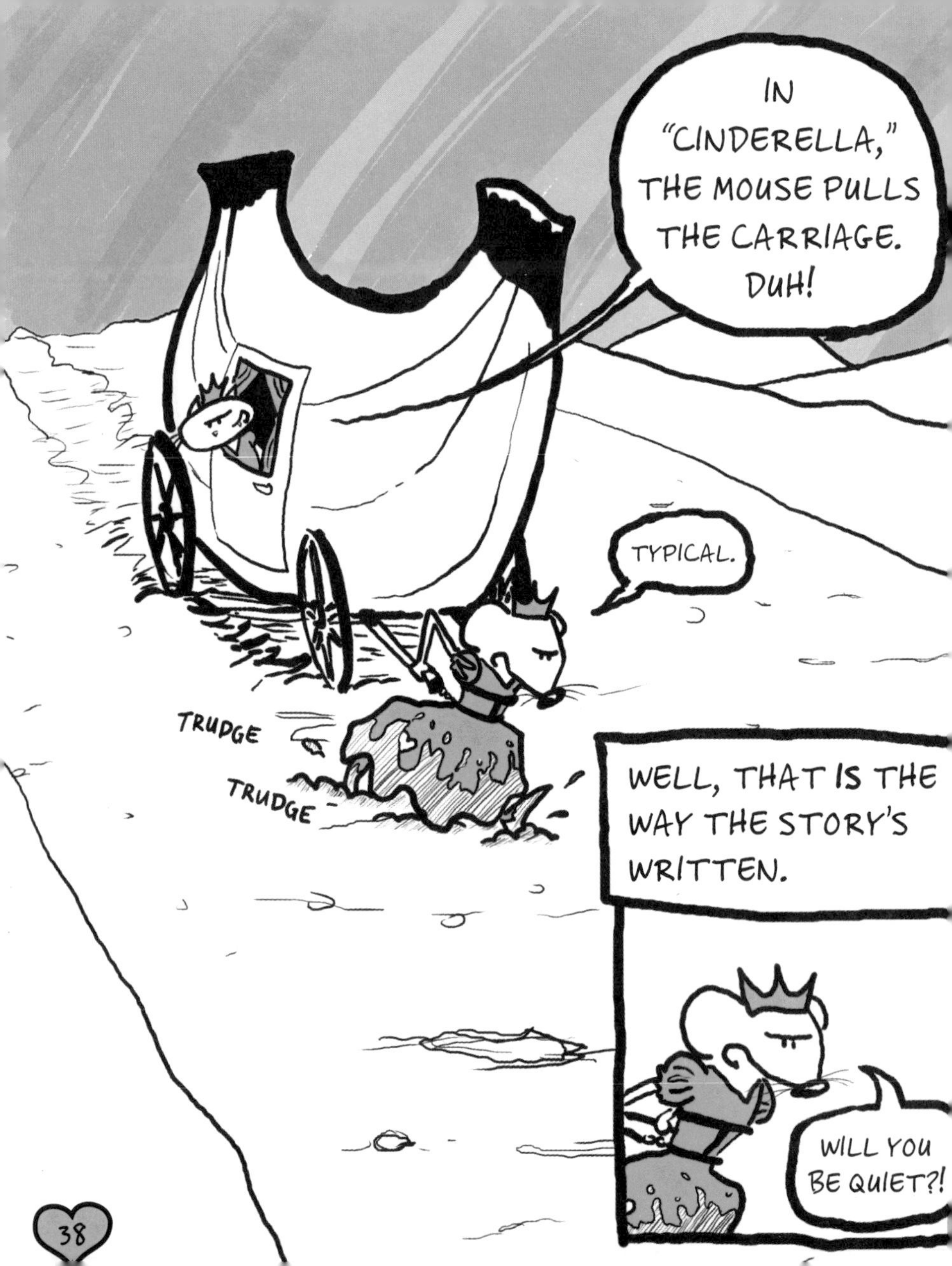
IN "CINDERELLA," THE MOUSE PULLS THE CARRIAGE. DUH!
TYPICAL.
TRUDGE
TRUDGE
WELL, THAT IS THE WAY THE STORY'S WRITTEN.
WILL YOU BE QUIET?!

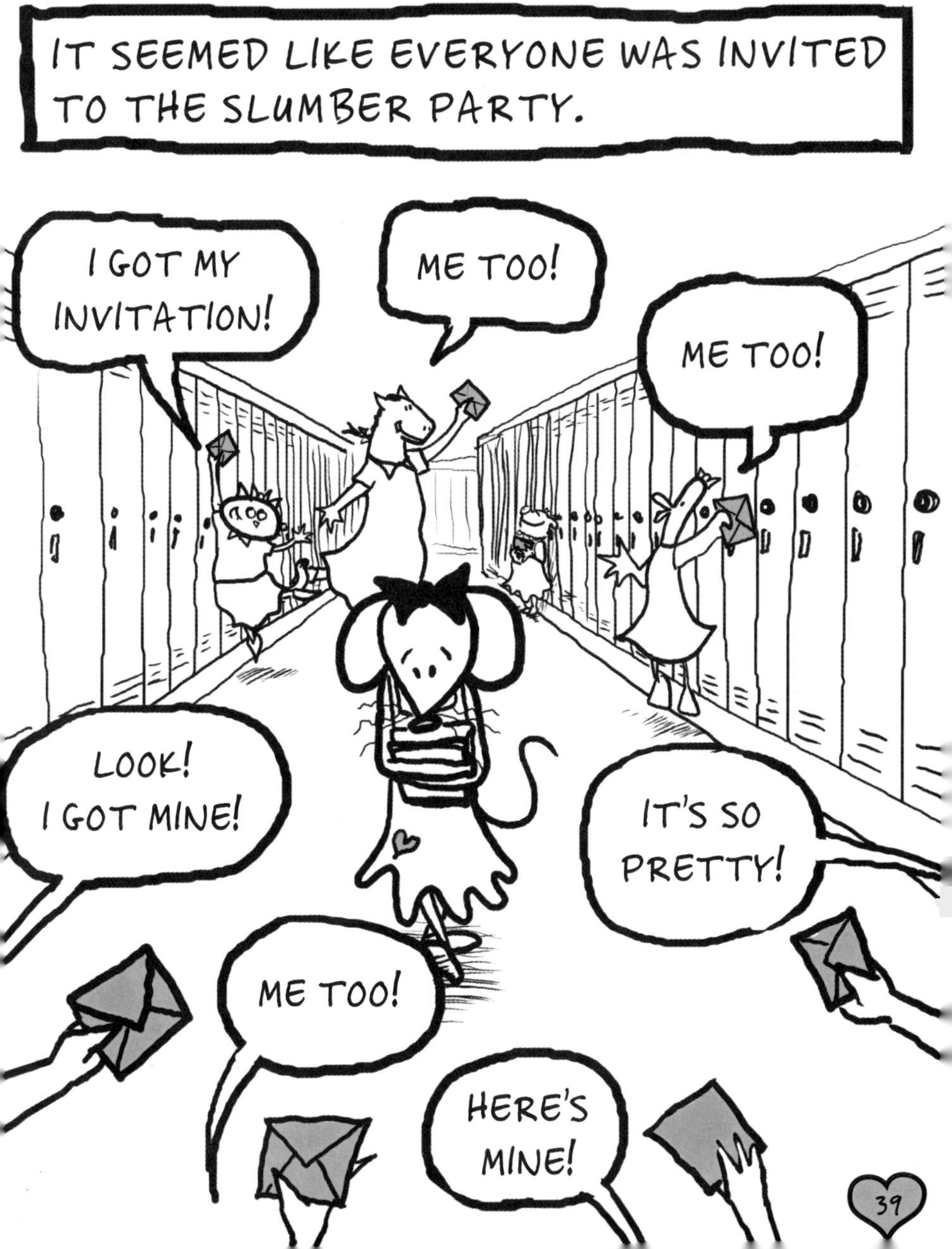
IT SEEMED LIKE EVERYONE WAS INVITED TO THE SLUMBER PARTY.
I GOT MY INVITATION!
ME TOO!
ME TOO!
LOOK! I GOT MINE!
IT'S SO PRETTY!
ME TOO!
HERE'S MINE!

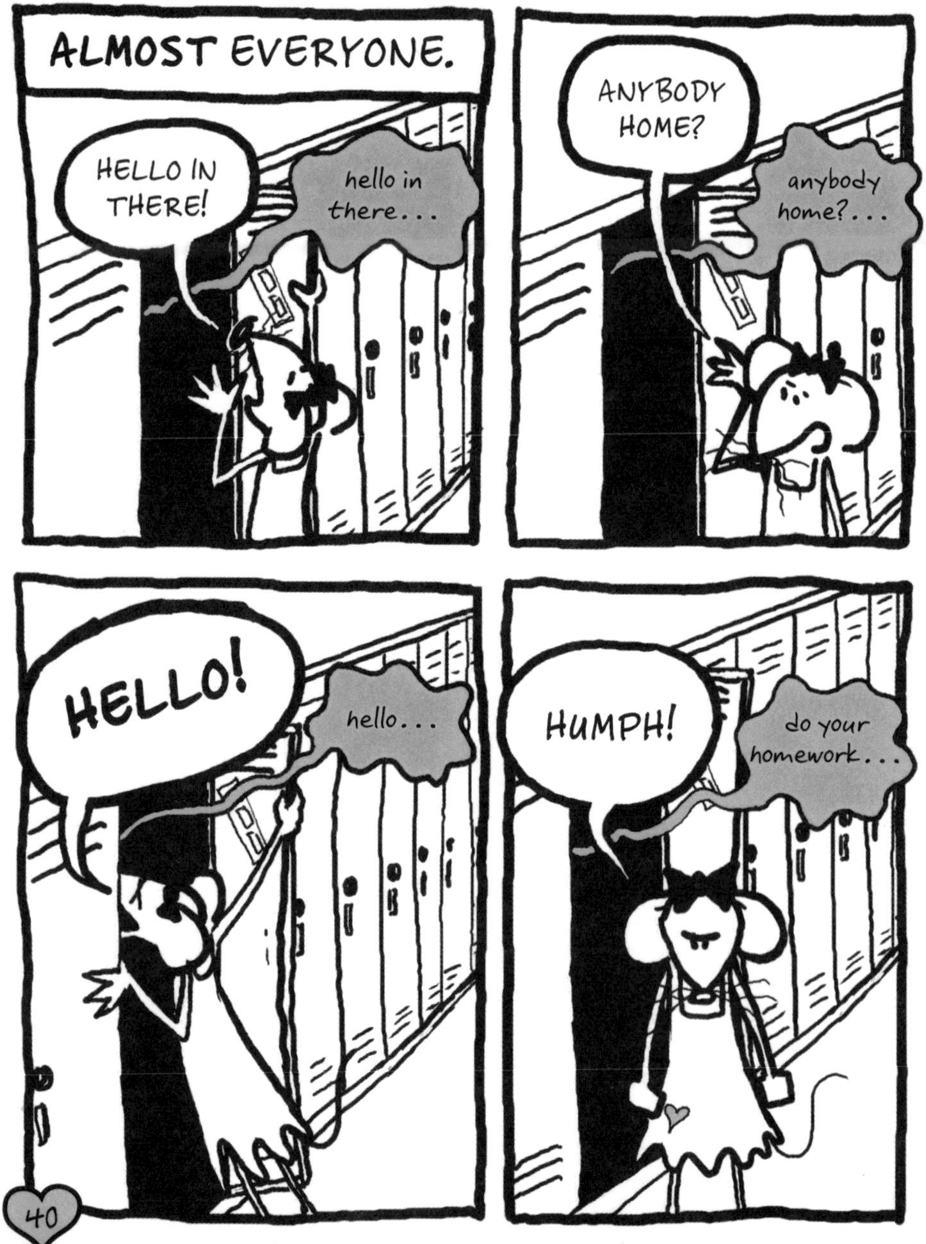
ALMOST EVERYONE.
HELLO IN THERE!
hello in there...
ANYBODY HOME?
anybody home?...
HELLO!
hello...
HUMPH!
do your homework...

BABYMOUSE KNEW THE SLUMBER PARTY WAS HER BIG CHANCE TO SHOW FELICIA FURRYPAWS HOW COOL SHE WAS!
...WHICH IS WHY MICE EAT CHEESE!
HA HA HA HA HA HA HA HA HA
HA HA HA HA HA HA HA HA
I NEVER KNEW HOW COOL SHE WAS!
SHE COULD SEE IT NOW.
PLEASE SAY YOU'LL BE MY BEST FRIEND.
I SUPPOSE.
HER WHOLE LIFE WOULD BE DIFFERENT.
HOW DO YOU GET YOUR WHISKERS SO CURLY?
THEY'RE NATURAL.
CAN I BORROW YOUR DRESS SOMETIME? THE HEART IS SO STYLISH!
I KNOW.

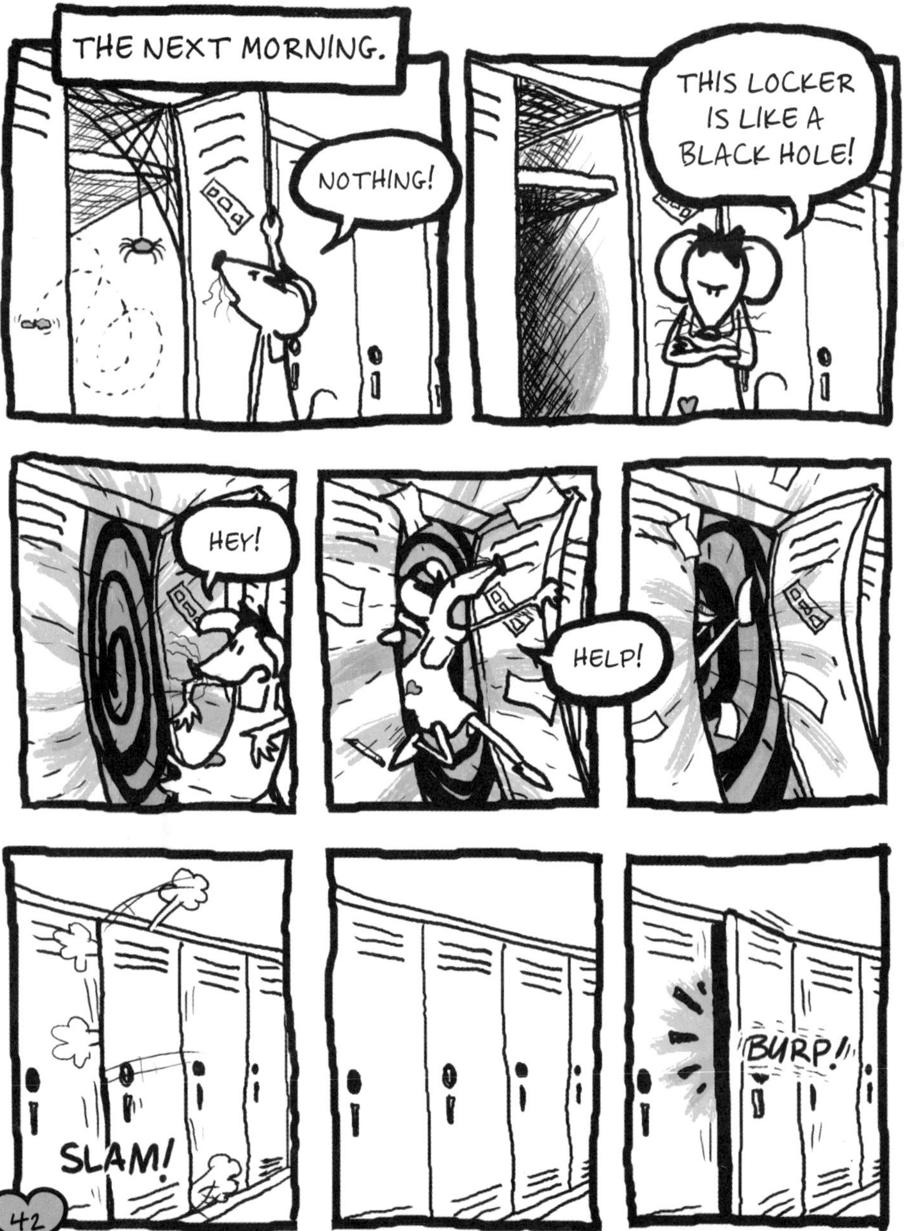
THE NEXT MORNING.
NOTHING!
THIS LOCKER IS LIKE A BLACK HOLE!
HEY!
HELP!
SLAM!
BURP!

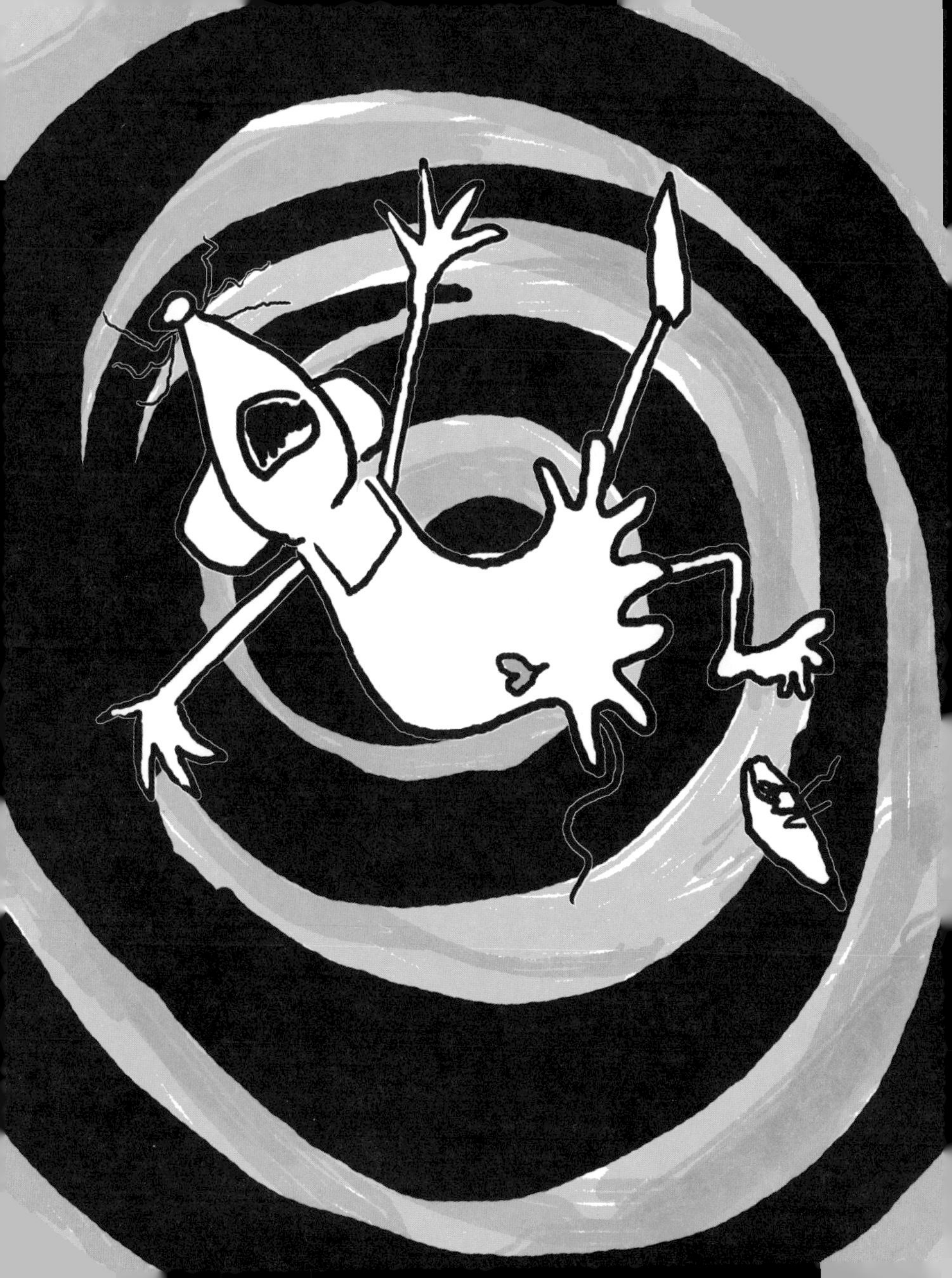

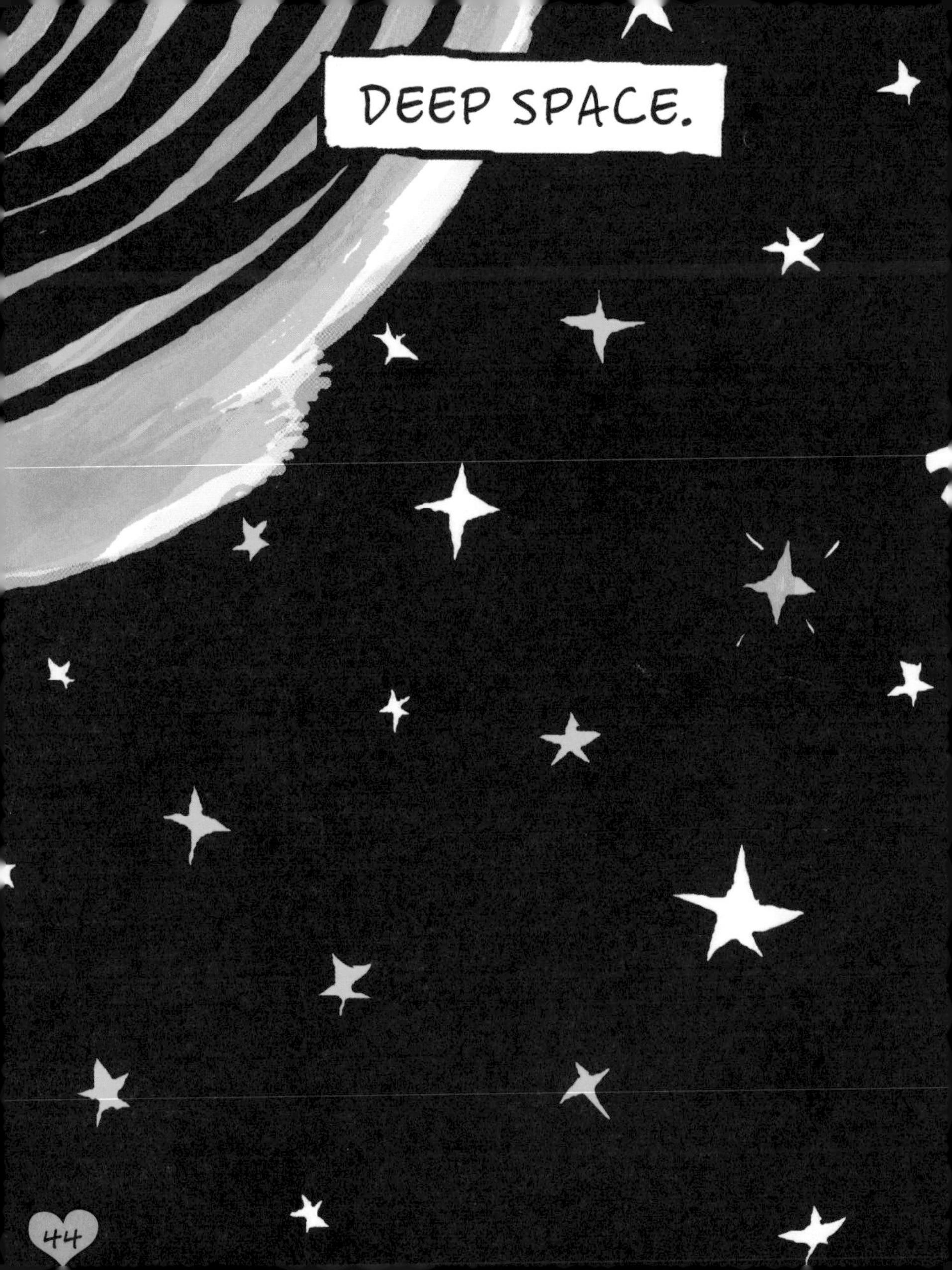
DEEP SPACE.

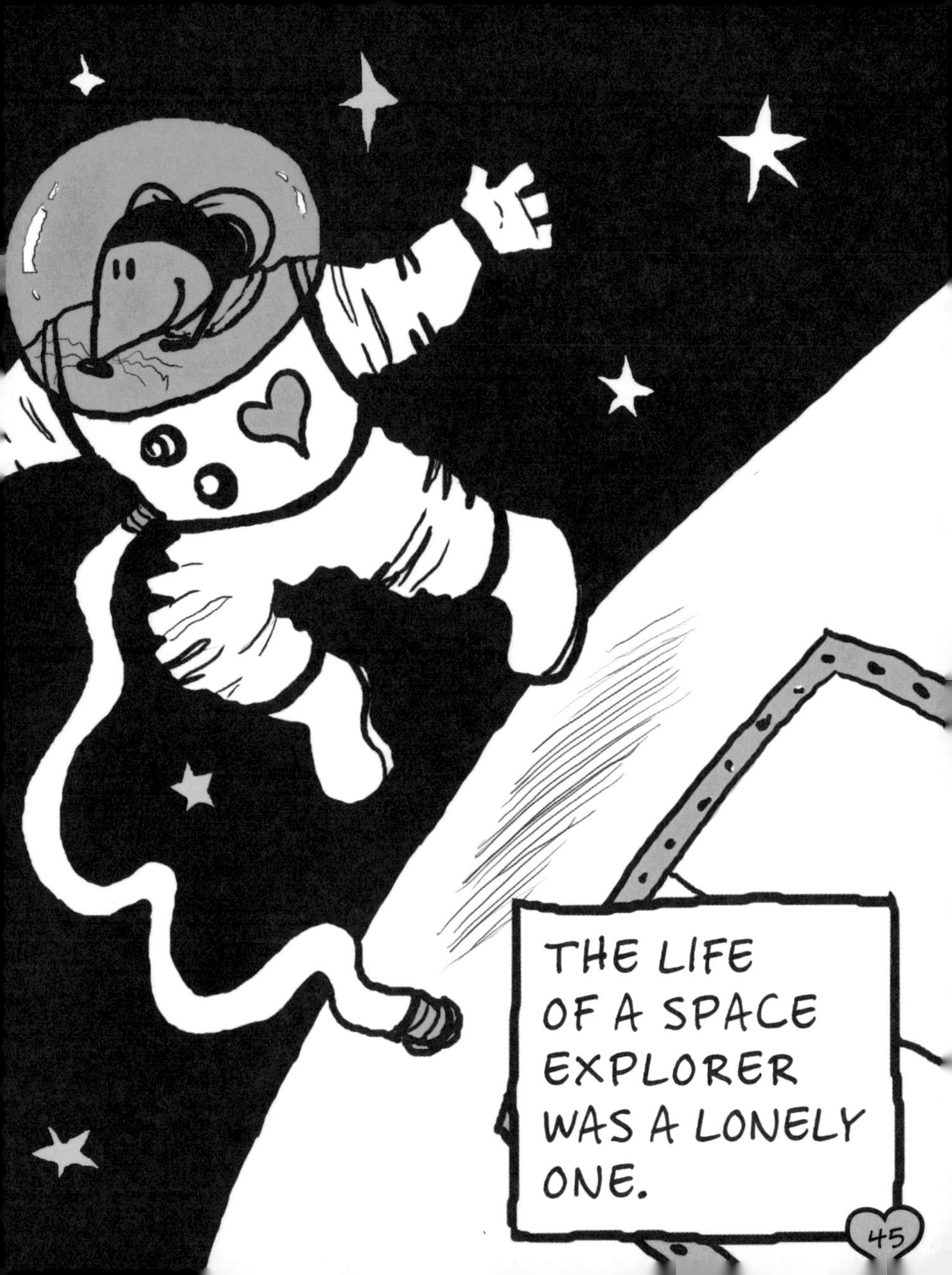
THE LIFE OF A SPACE EXPLORER WAS A LONELY ONE.

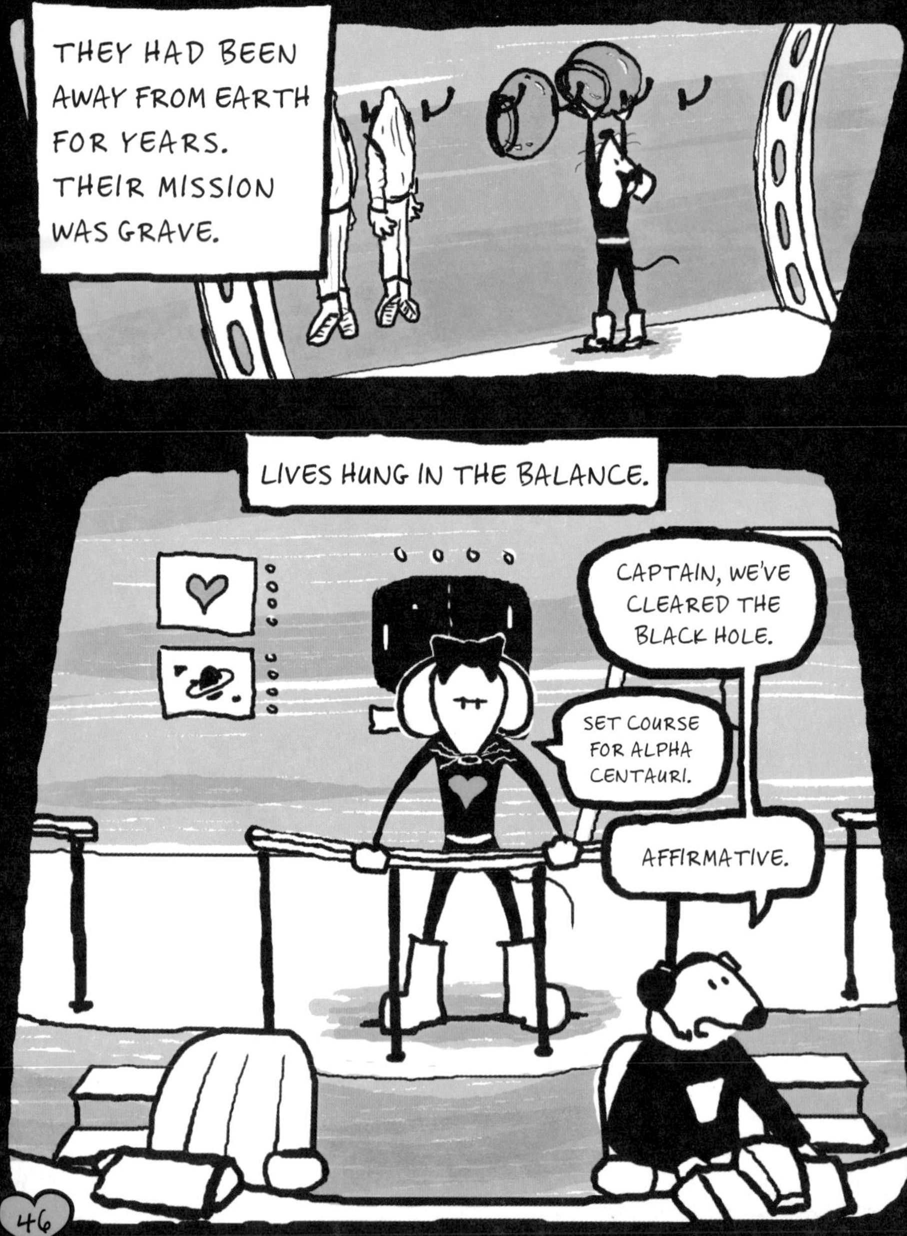
THEY HAD BEEN AWAY FROM EARTH FOR YEARS. THEIR MISSION WAS GRAVE.
LIVES HUNG IN THE BALANCE.
CAPTAIN, WE'VE CLEARED THE BLACK HOLE.
SET COURSE FOR ALPHA CENTAURI.
AFFIRMATIVE.

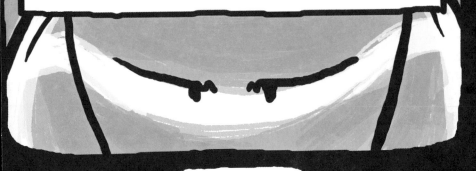

THEY DARED NOT FAIL.

THERE IT IS, CAPTAIN!

FINALLY, AFTER ALL THESE YEARS...

WE'VE FOUND WHAT WE'VE SEARCHED THE GALAXY FOR!

ALIEN LIFE, CAPTAIN?

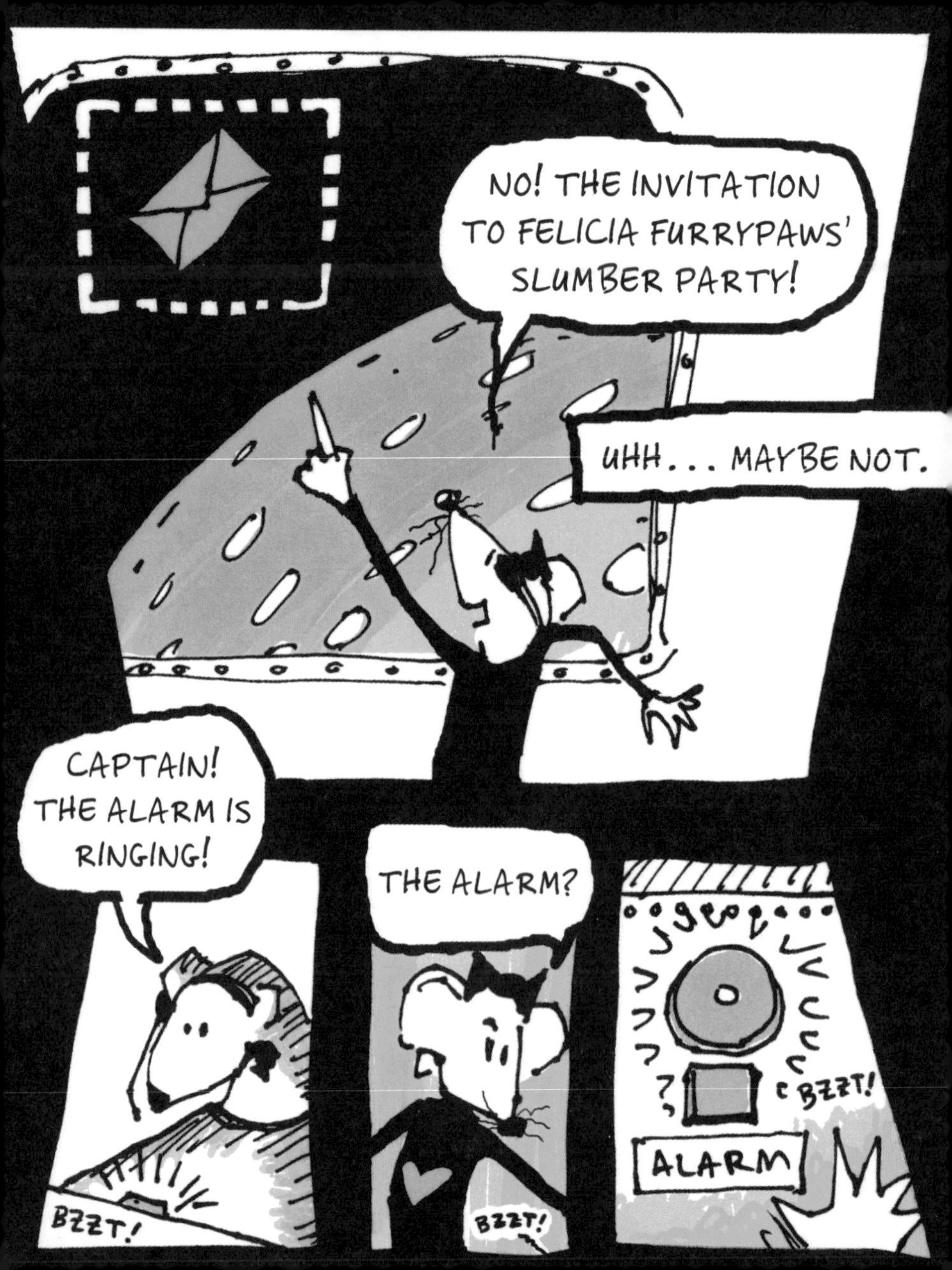
NO! THE INVITATION TO FELICIA FURRYPAWS' SLUMBER PARTY!
UHH... MAYBE NOT.
CAPTAIN! THE ALARM IS RINGING!
BZZT!
THE ALARM?
BZZT!
BZZT!
ALARM

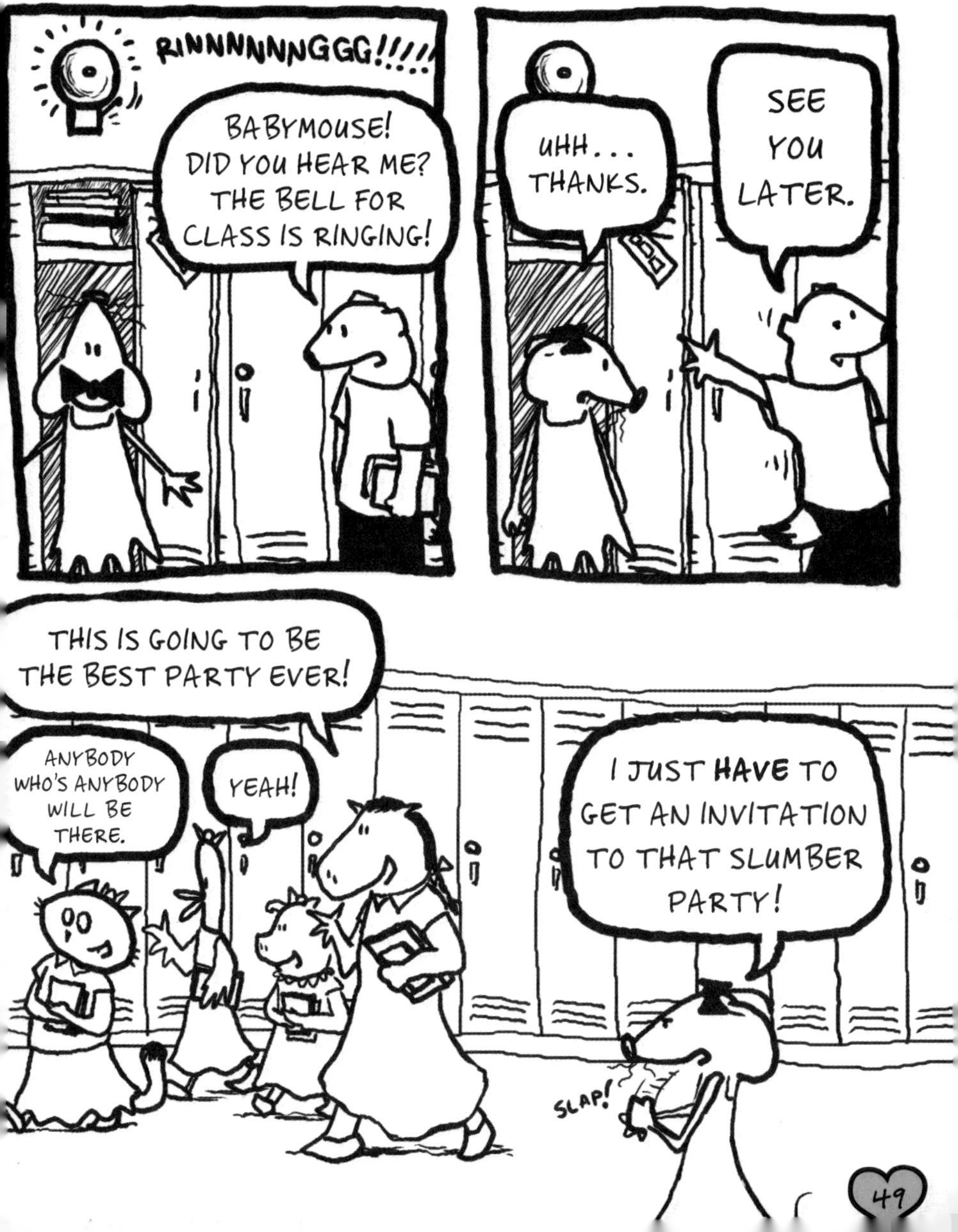
RINNNNNNGGG!!!!
BABYMOUSE! DID YOU HEAR ME? THE BELL FOR CLASS IS RINGING!
UHH... THANKS.
SEE YOU LATER.
THIS IS GOING TO BE THE BEST PARTY EVER!
ANYBODY WHO'S ANYBODY WILL BE THERE.
YEAH!
I JUST **HAVE** TO GET AN INVITATION TO THAT SLUMBER PARTY!
SLAP!

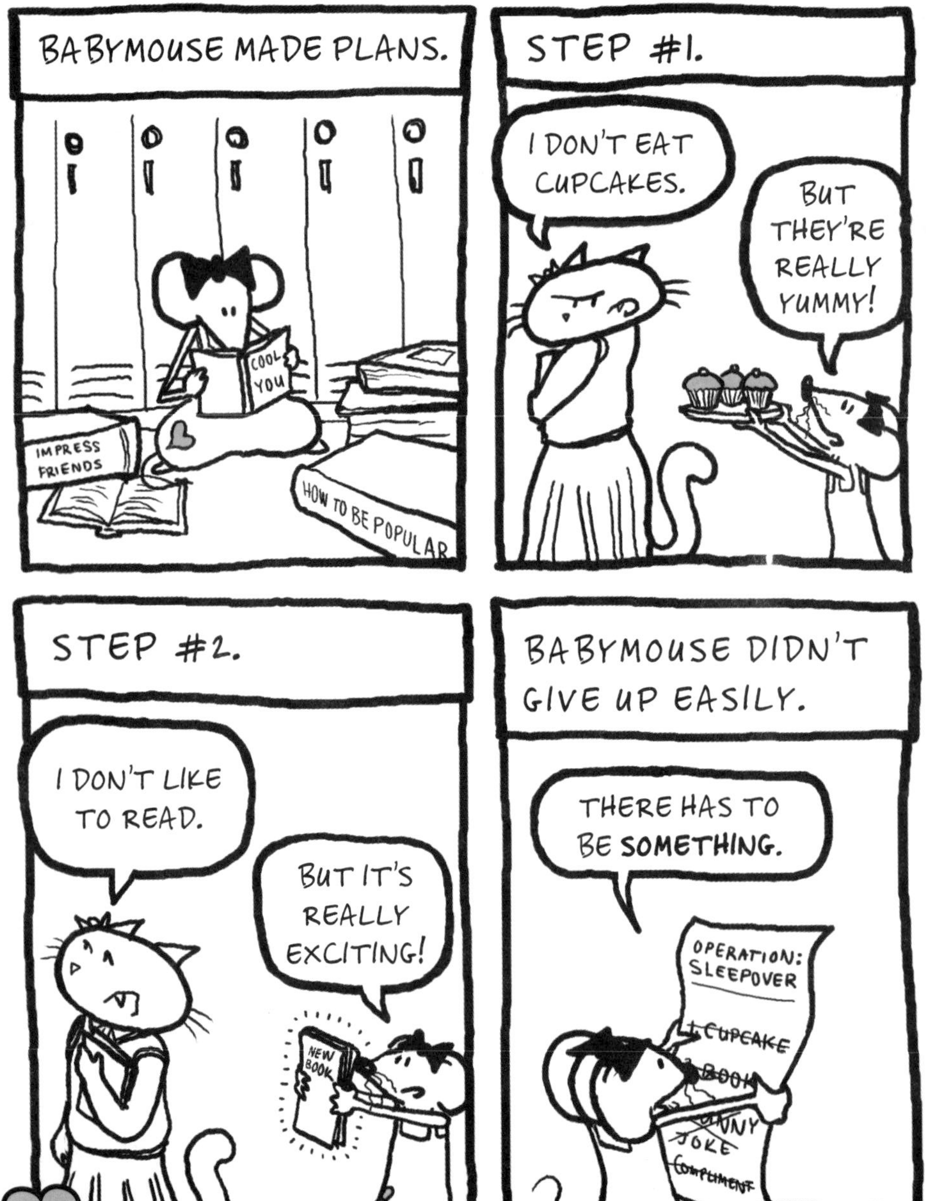

BABYMOUSE MADE PLANS.
COOL YOU
IMPRESS FRIENDS
HOW TO BE POPULAR
STEP #1.
I DON'T EAT CUPCAKES.
BUT THEY'RE REALLY YUMMY!
STEP #2.
I DON'T LIKE TO READ.
BUT IT'S REALLY EXCITING!
NEW BOOK
BABYMOUSE DIDN'T GIVE UP EASILY.
THERE HAS TO BE **SOMETHING.**
OPERATION: SLEEPOVER
1. CUPCAKE
BOOK
JOKE
COMPLIMENT

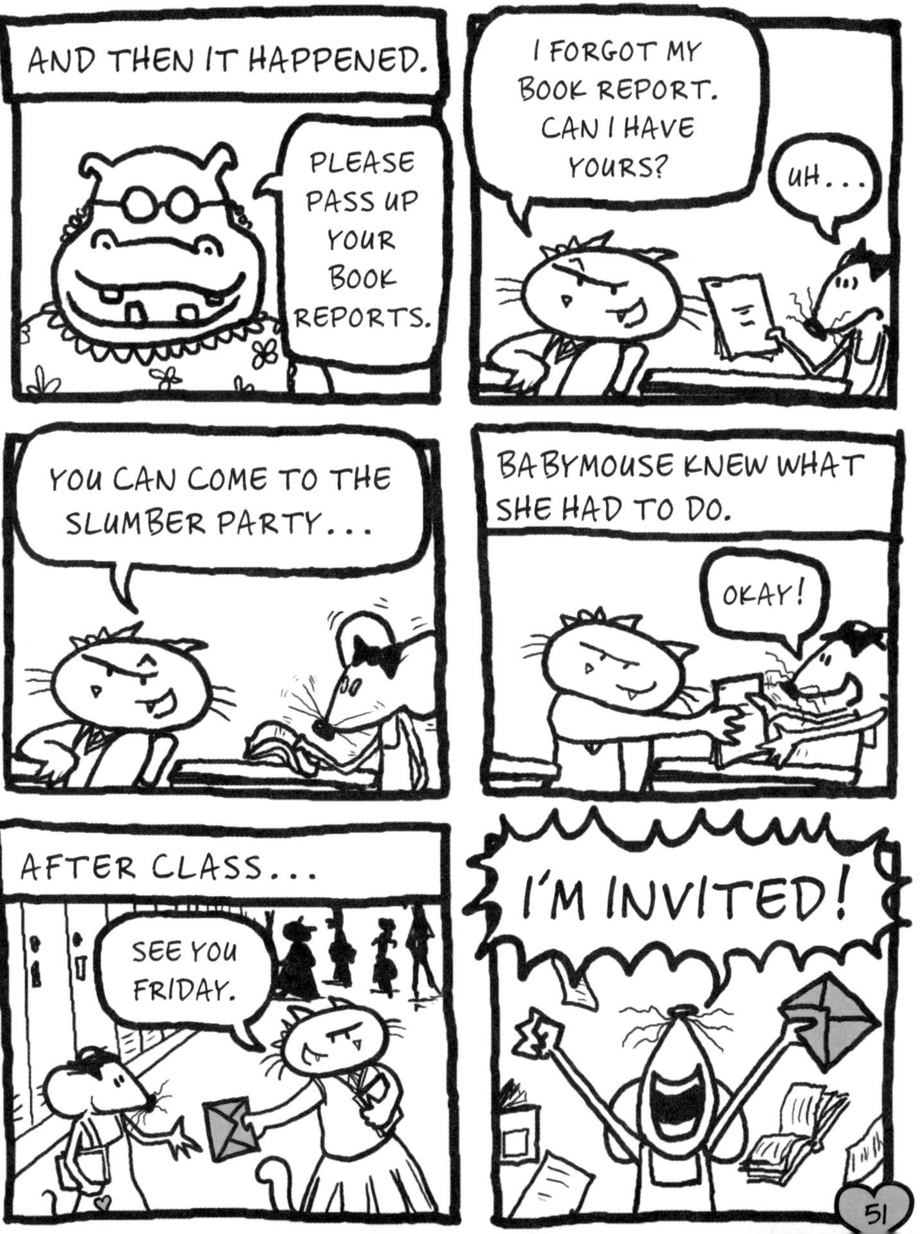
AND THEN IT HAPPENED.
PLEASE PASS UP YOUR BOOK REPORTS.
I FORGOT MY BOOK REPORT. CAN I HAVE YOURS?
UH...
YOU CAN COME TO THE SLUMBER PARTY...
BABYMOUSE KNEW WHAT SHE HAD TO DO.
OKAY!
AFTER CLASS...
SEE YOU FRIDAY.
I'M INVITED!

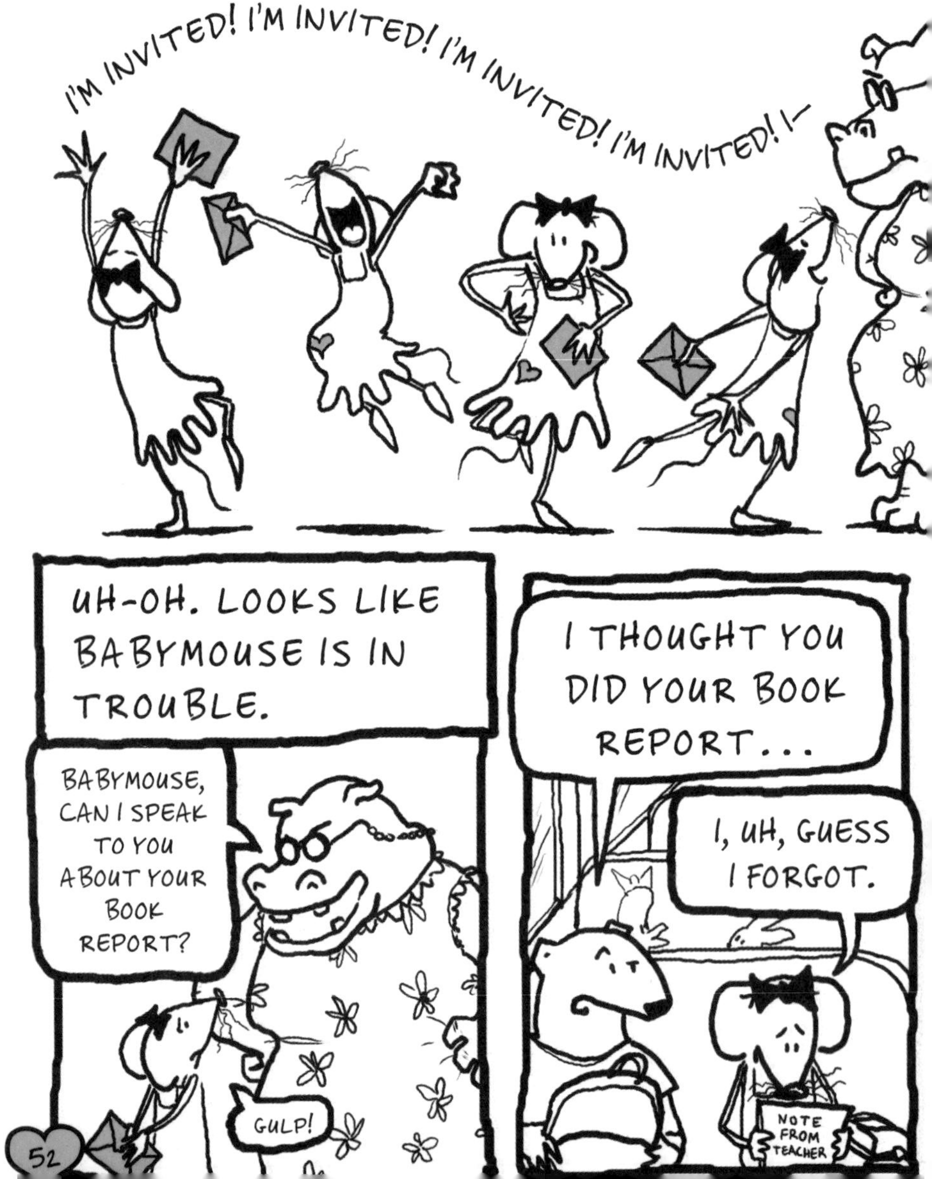
I'M INVITED! I'M INVITED! I'M INVITED! I'M INVITED! I—
UH-OH. LOOKS LIKE BABYMOUSE IS IN TROUBLE.
BABYMOUSE, CAN I SPEAK TO YOU ABOUT YOUR BOOK REPORT?
GULP!
I THOUGHT YOU DID YOUR BOOK REPORT...
I, UH, GUESS I FORGOT.
NOTE FROM TEACHER

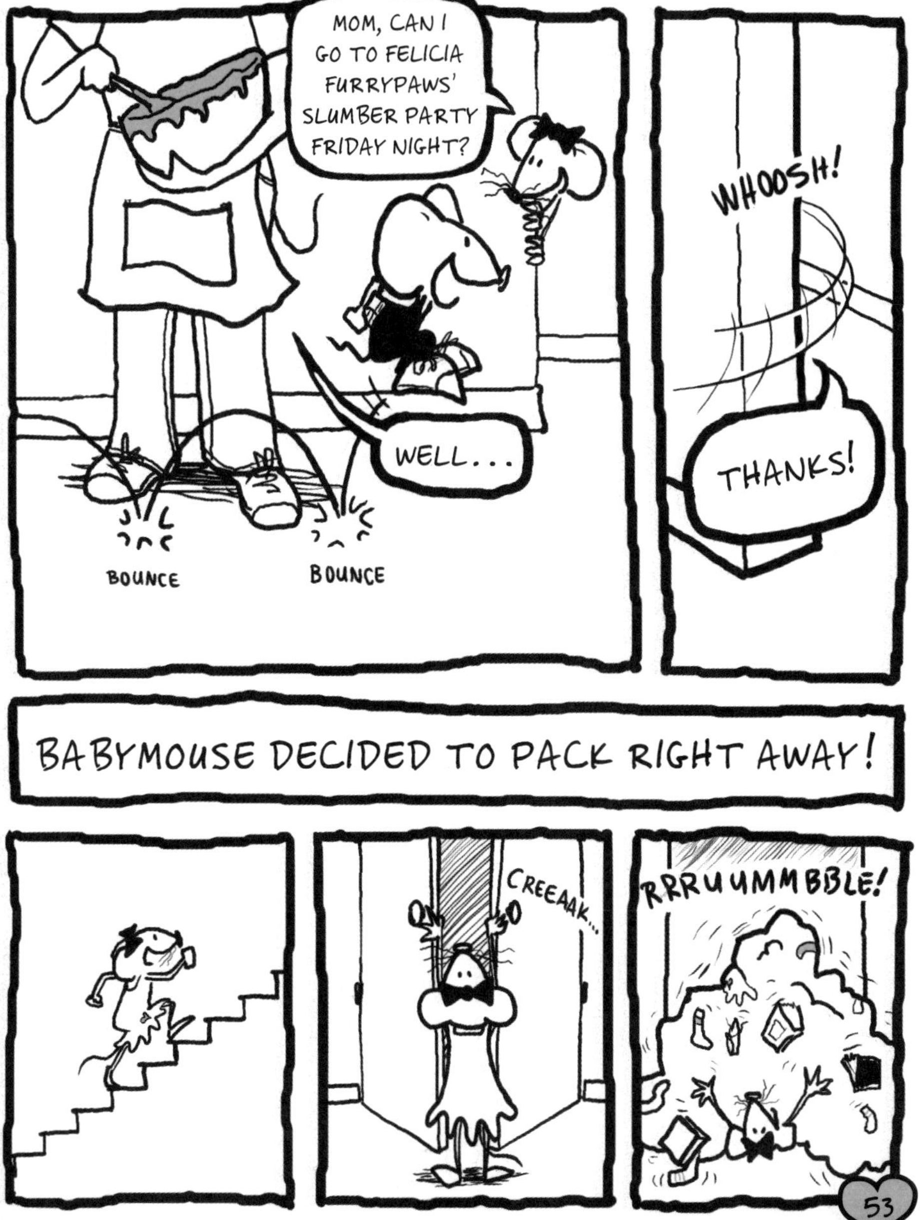
MOM, CAN I GO TO FELICIA FURRYPAWS' SLUMBER PARTY FRIDAY NIGHT?
WELL...
BOUNCE
BOUNCE
WHOOSH!
THANKS!
BABYMOUSE DECIDED TO PACK RIGHT AWAY!
CREEAAK...
RRRUUMMBBLE!

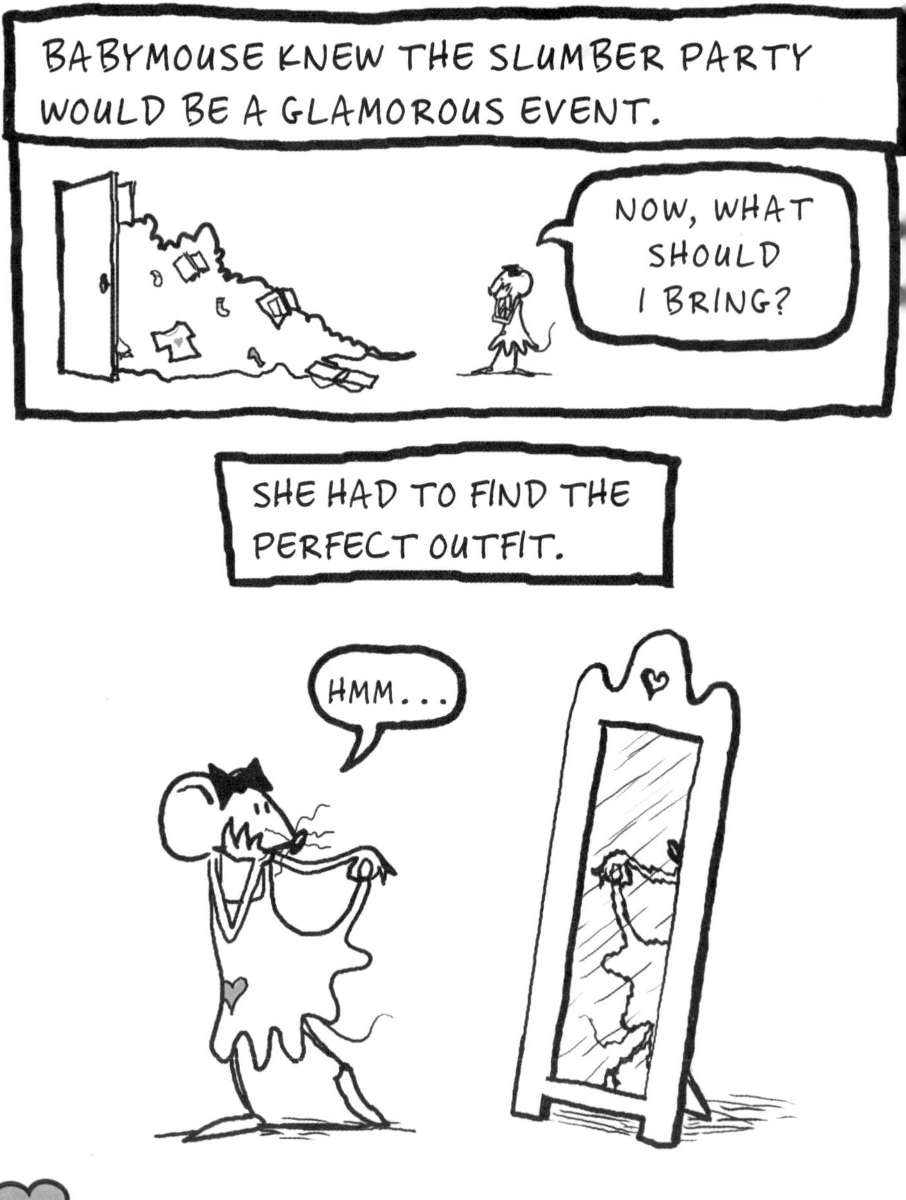
BABYMOUSE KNEW THE SLUMBER PARTY WOULD BE A GLAMOROUS EVENT.
NOW, WHAT SHOULD I BRING?
SHE HAD TO FIND THE PERFECT OUTFIT.
HMM...

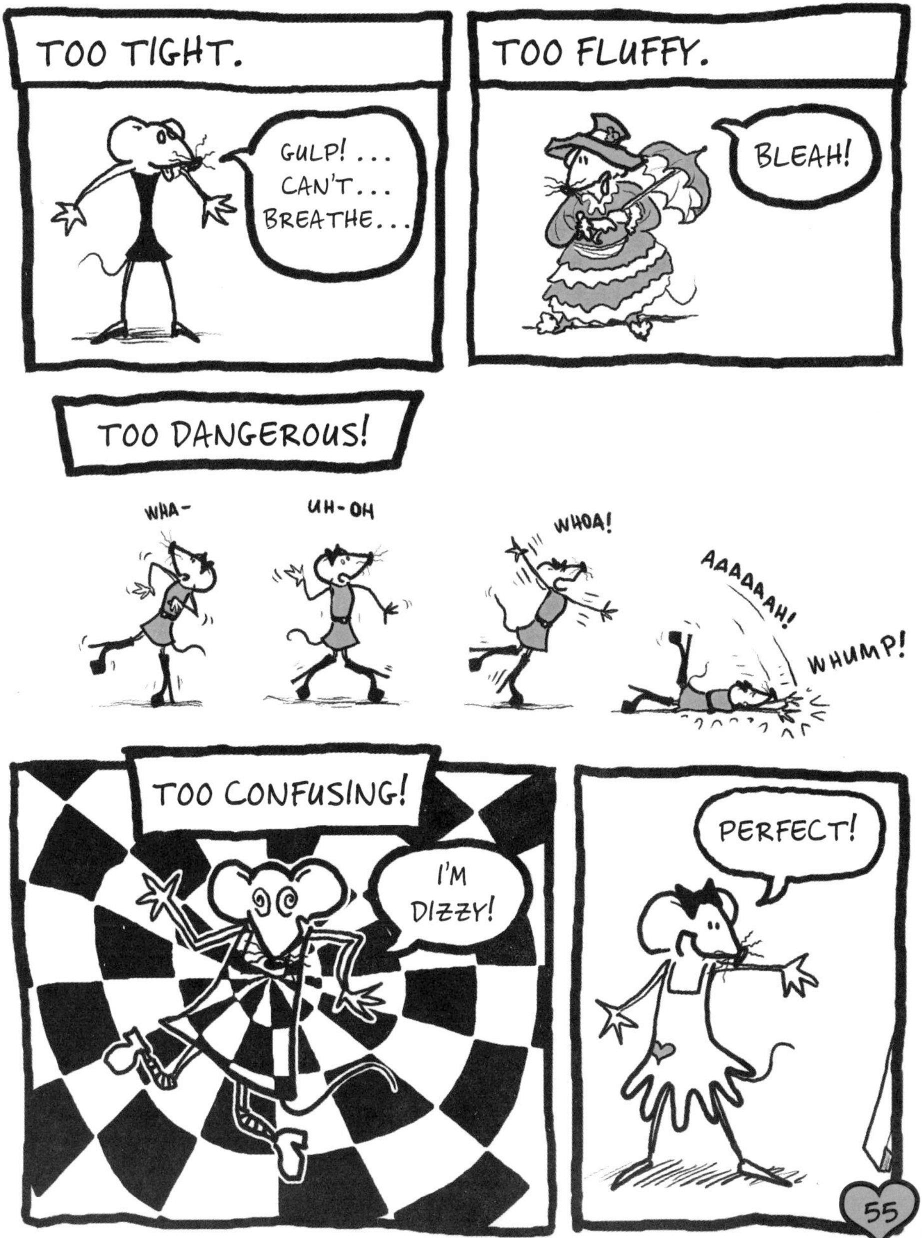
TOO TIGHT.
GULP! . . . CAN'T . . . BREATHE . . .
TOO FLUFFY.
BLEAH!
TOO DANGEROUS!
WHA-
UH-OH
WHOA!
AAAAAAAH!
WHUMP!
TOO CONFUSING!
I'M DIZZY!
PERFECT!

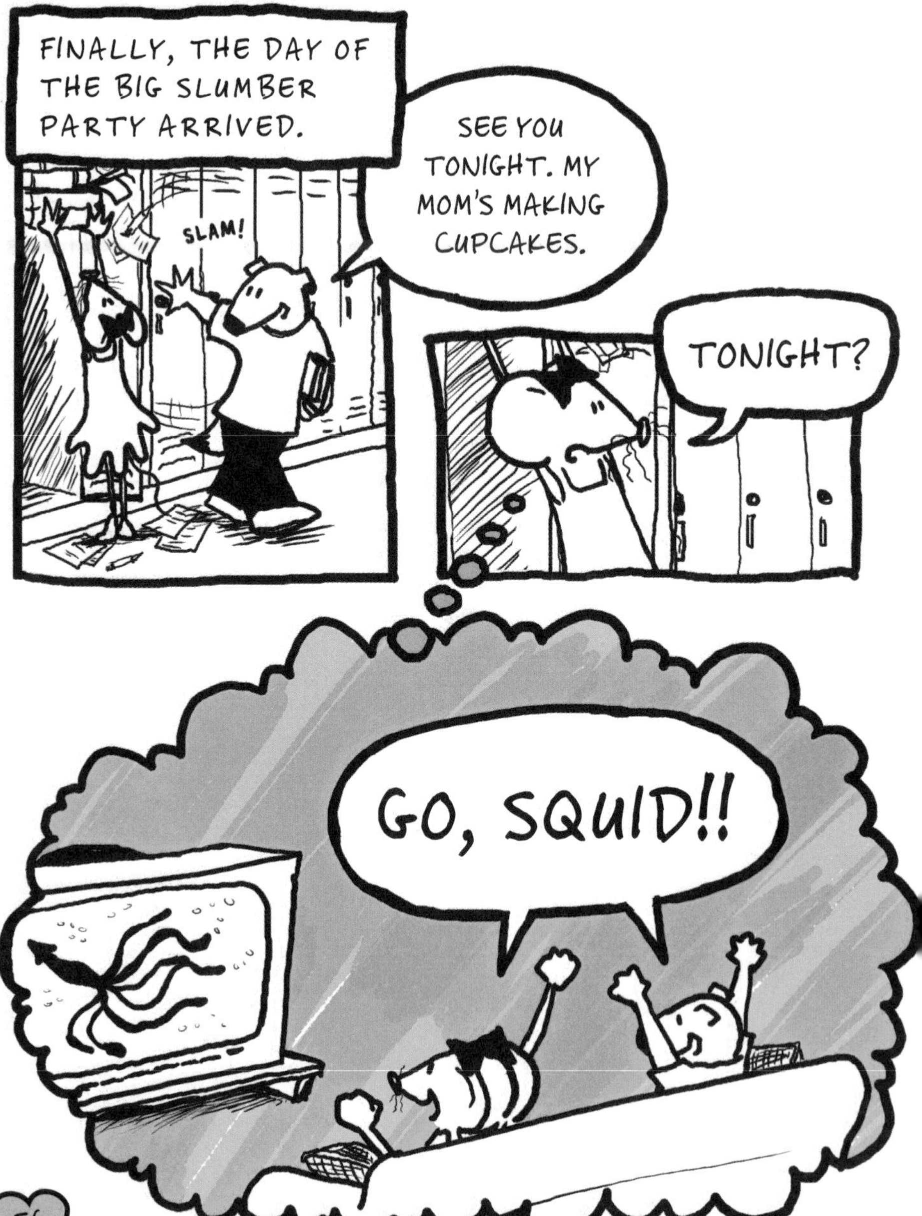
FINALLY, THE DAY OF THE BIG SLUMBER PARTY ARRIVED.
SLAM!
SEE YOU TONIGHT. MY MOM'S MAKING CUPCAKES.
TONIGHT?
GO, SQUID!!

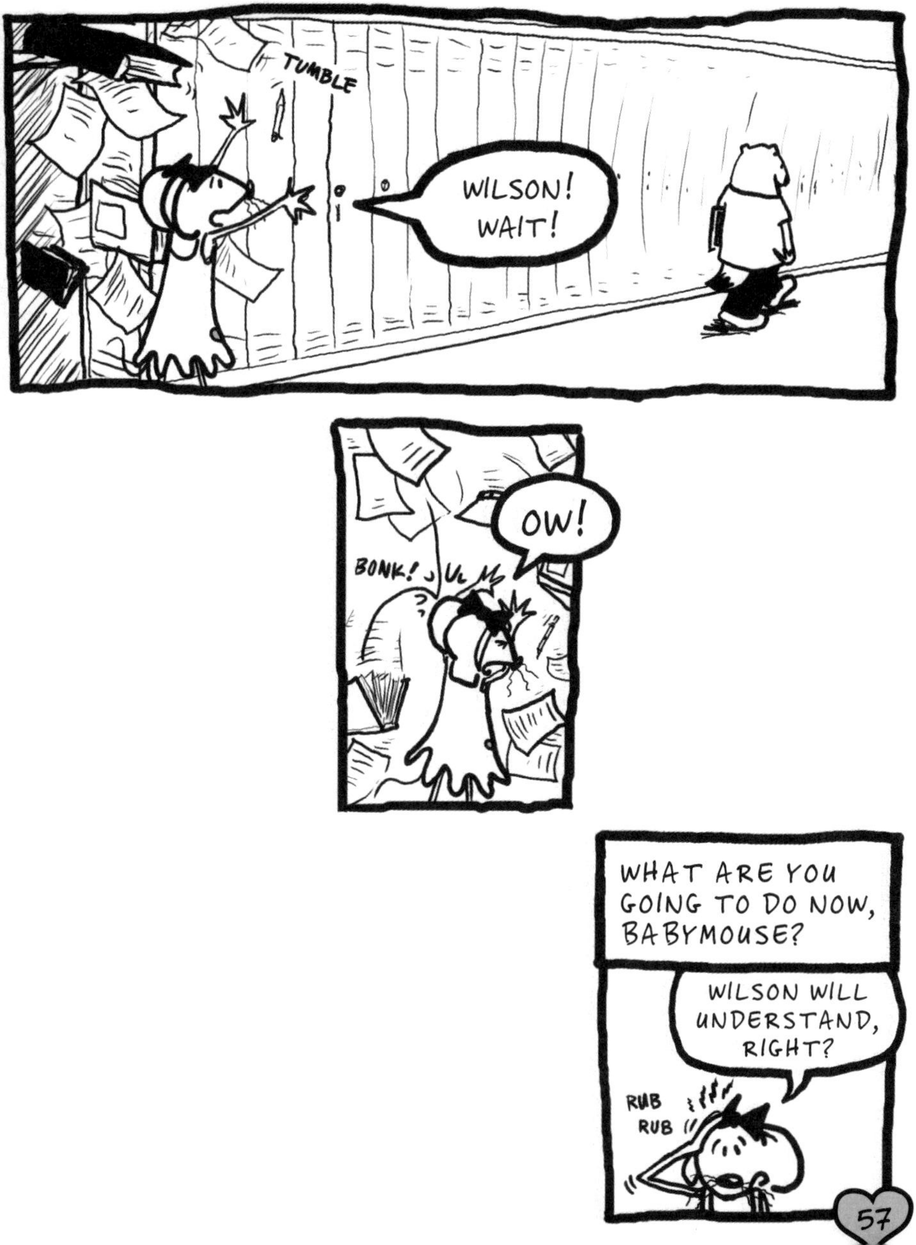
TUMBLE
WILSON! WAIT!
BONK!
OW!
WHAT ARE YOU GOING TO DO NOW, BABYMOUSE?
WILSON WILL UNDERSTAND, RIGHT?
RUB RUB

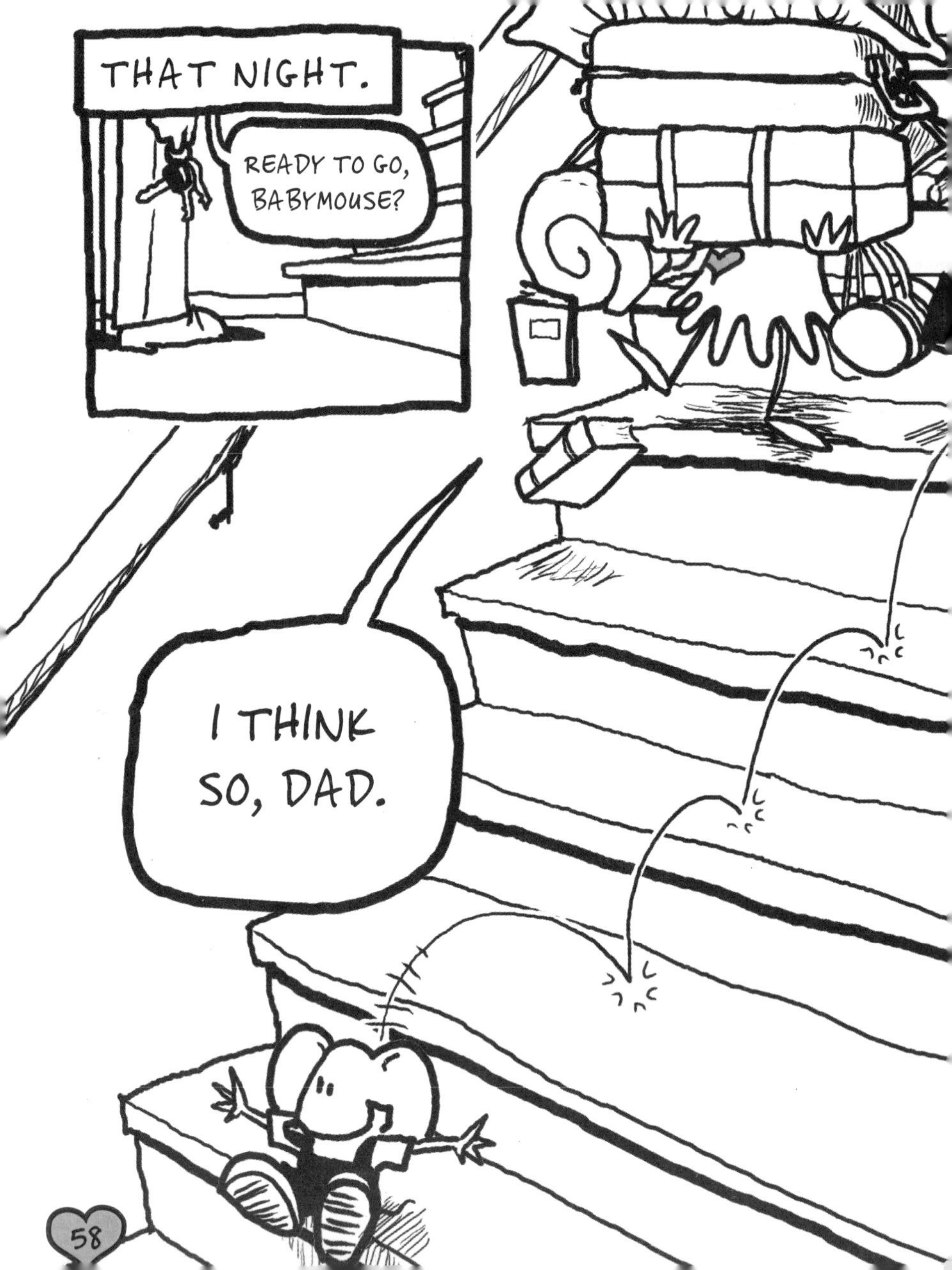
THAT NIGHT.
READY TO GO, BABYMOUSE?
I THINK SO, DAD.

BABYMOUSE WAS EXCITED THE WHOLE WAY OVER TO FELICIA'S.

SHE HAD LOTS OF IDEAS ABOUT WHAT THEY WERE GOING TO DO.

SKYDIVING!

DINNER THEATER!

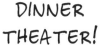

GO-KART RACING!

SNORKELING!

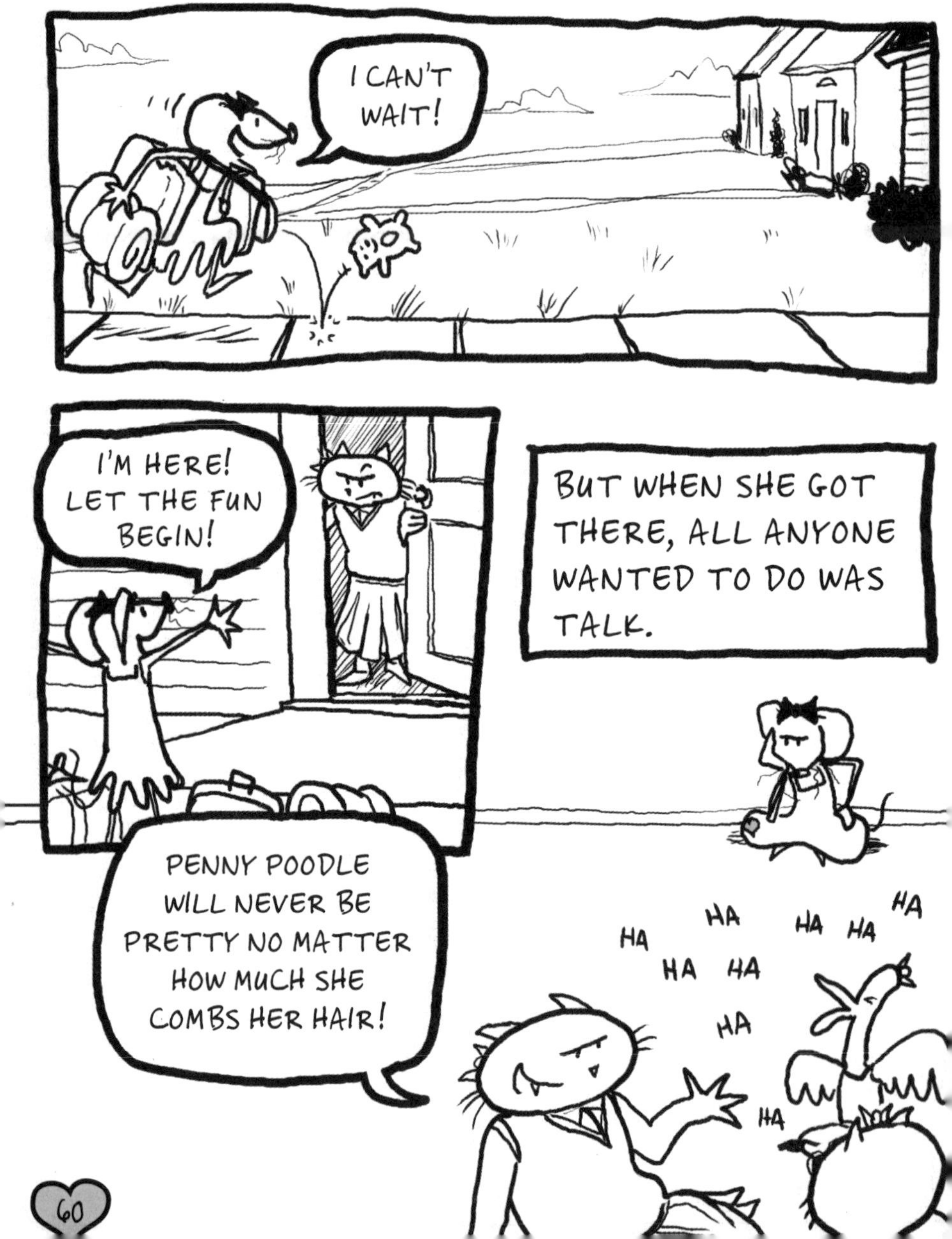
I CAN'T WAIT!
I'M HERE! LET THE FUN BEGIN!
BUT WHEN SHE GOT THERE, ALL ANYONE WANTED TO DO WAS TALK.
PENNY POODLE WILL NEVER BE PRETTY NO MATTER HOW MUCH SHE COMBS HER HAIR!
HA HA HA HA HA HA HA HA HA HA

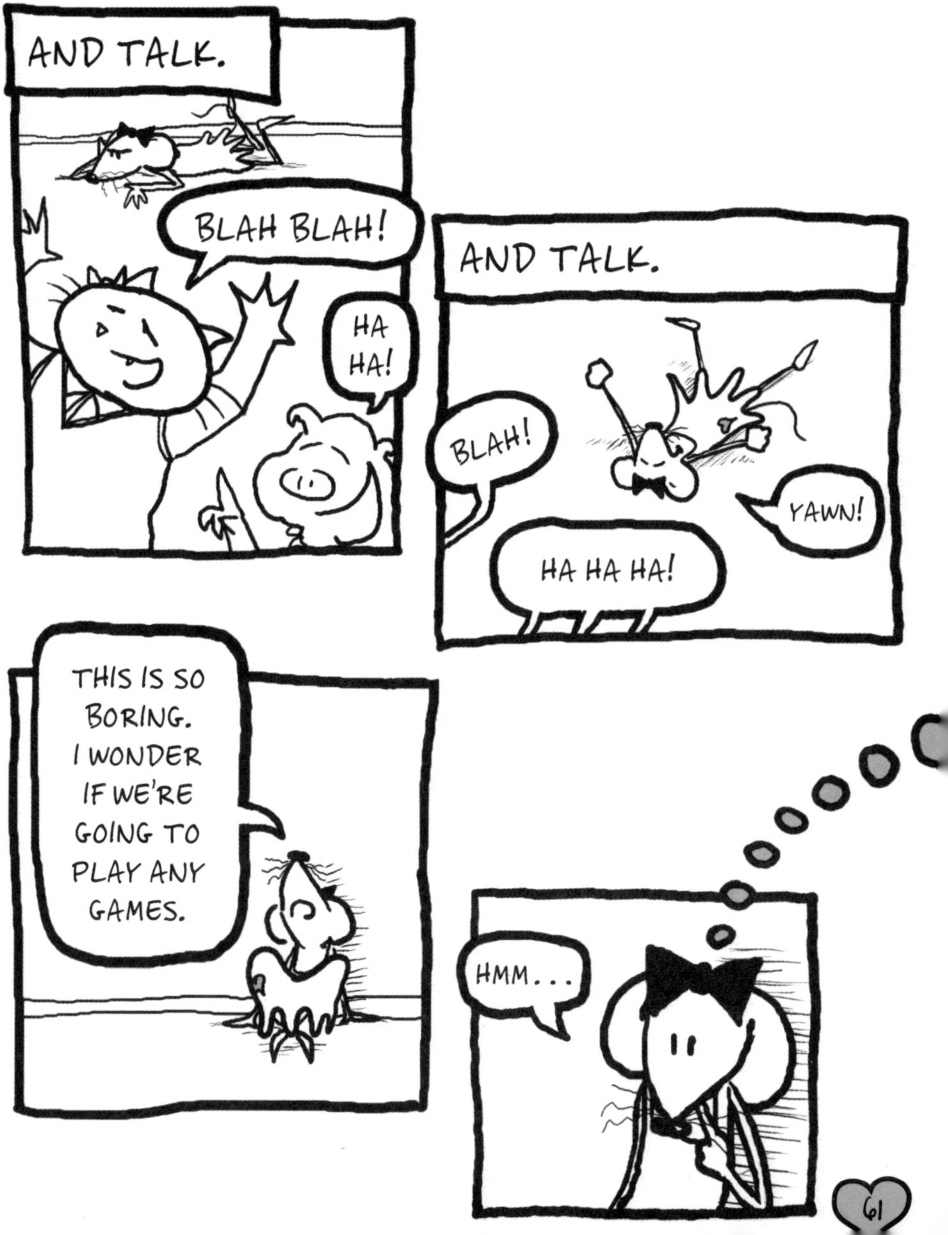
AND TALK.
BLAH BLAH!
HA HA!
AND TALK.
BLAH!
YAWN!
HA HA HA!
THIS IS SO BORING. I WONDER IF WE'RE GOING TO PLAY ANY GAMES.
HMM...

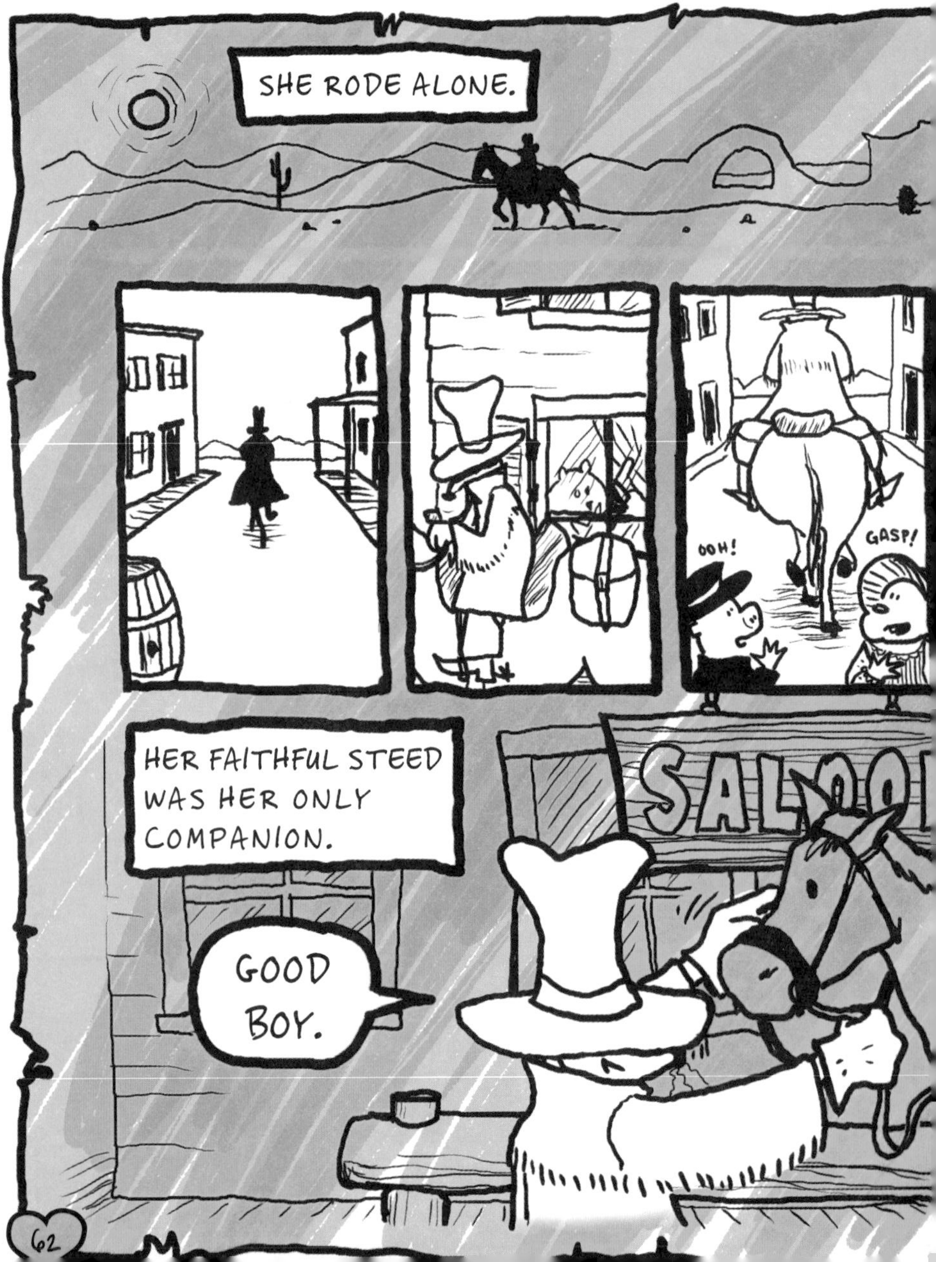
SHE RODE ALONE.
OOH!
GASP!
HER FAITHFUL STEED WAS HER ONLY COMPANION.
SALOO
GOOD BOY.

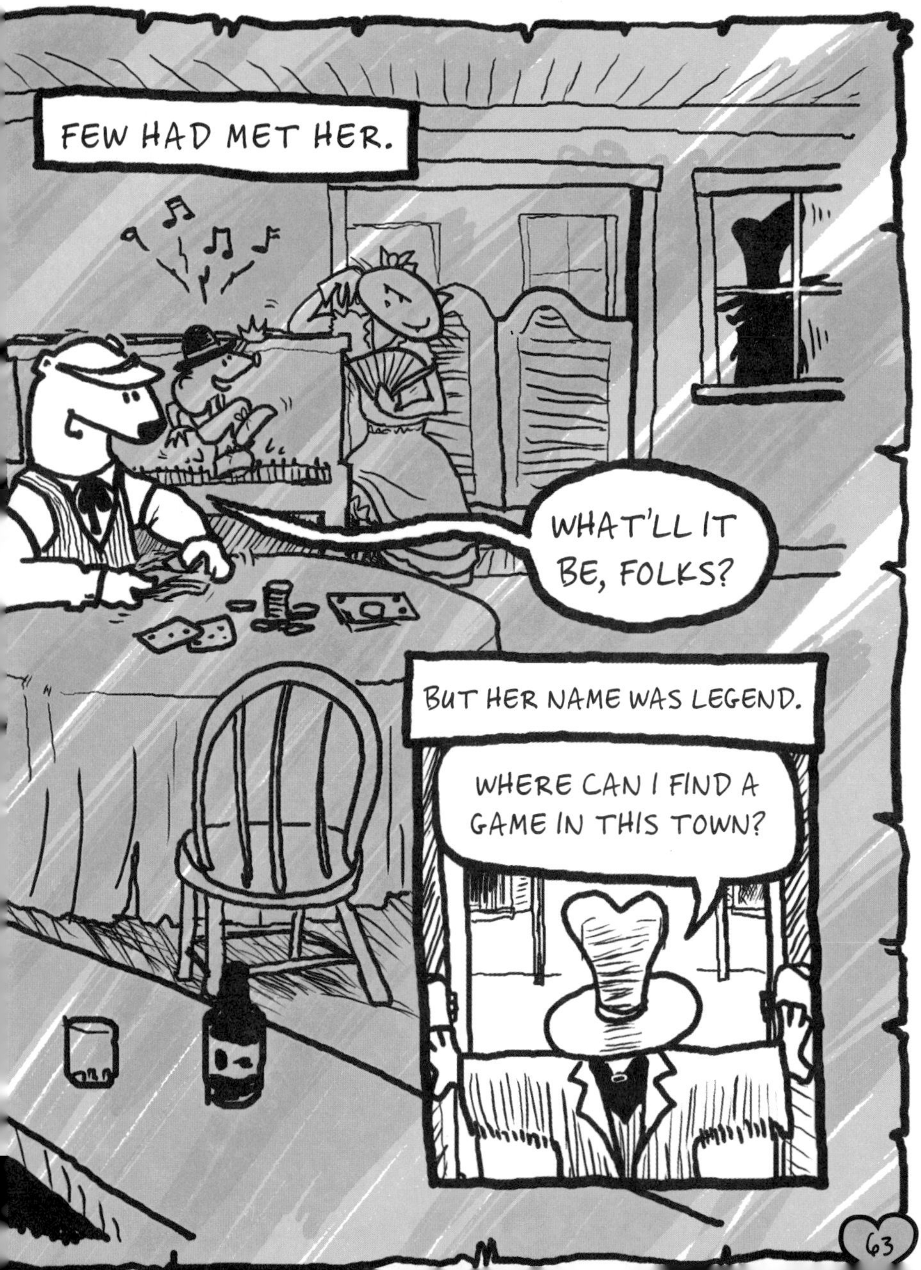
FEW HAD MET HER.
WHAT'LL IT BE, FOLKS?
BUT HER NAME WAS LEGEND.
WHERE CAN I FIND A GAME IN THIS TOWN?

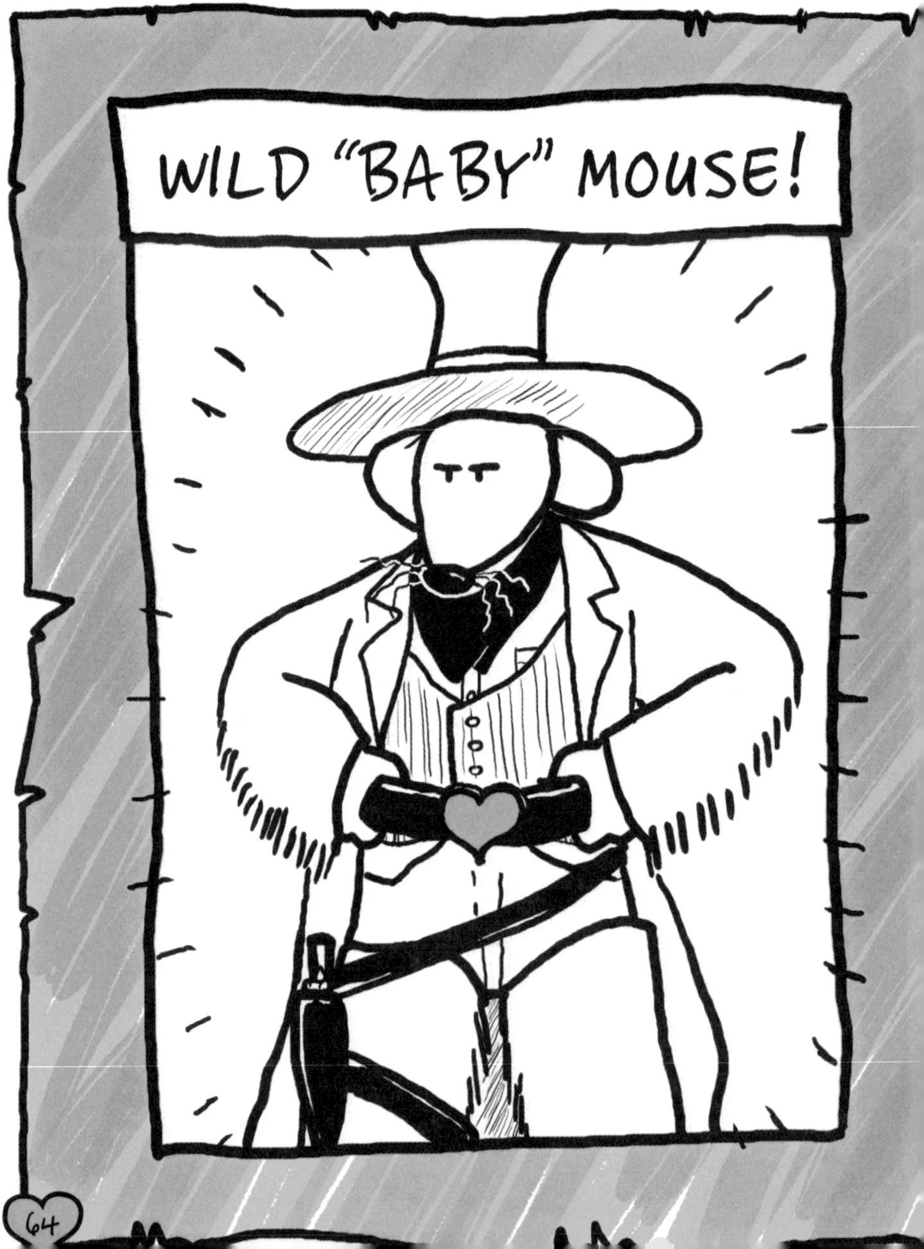
WILD "BABY" MOUSE!

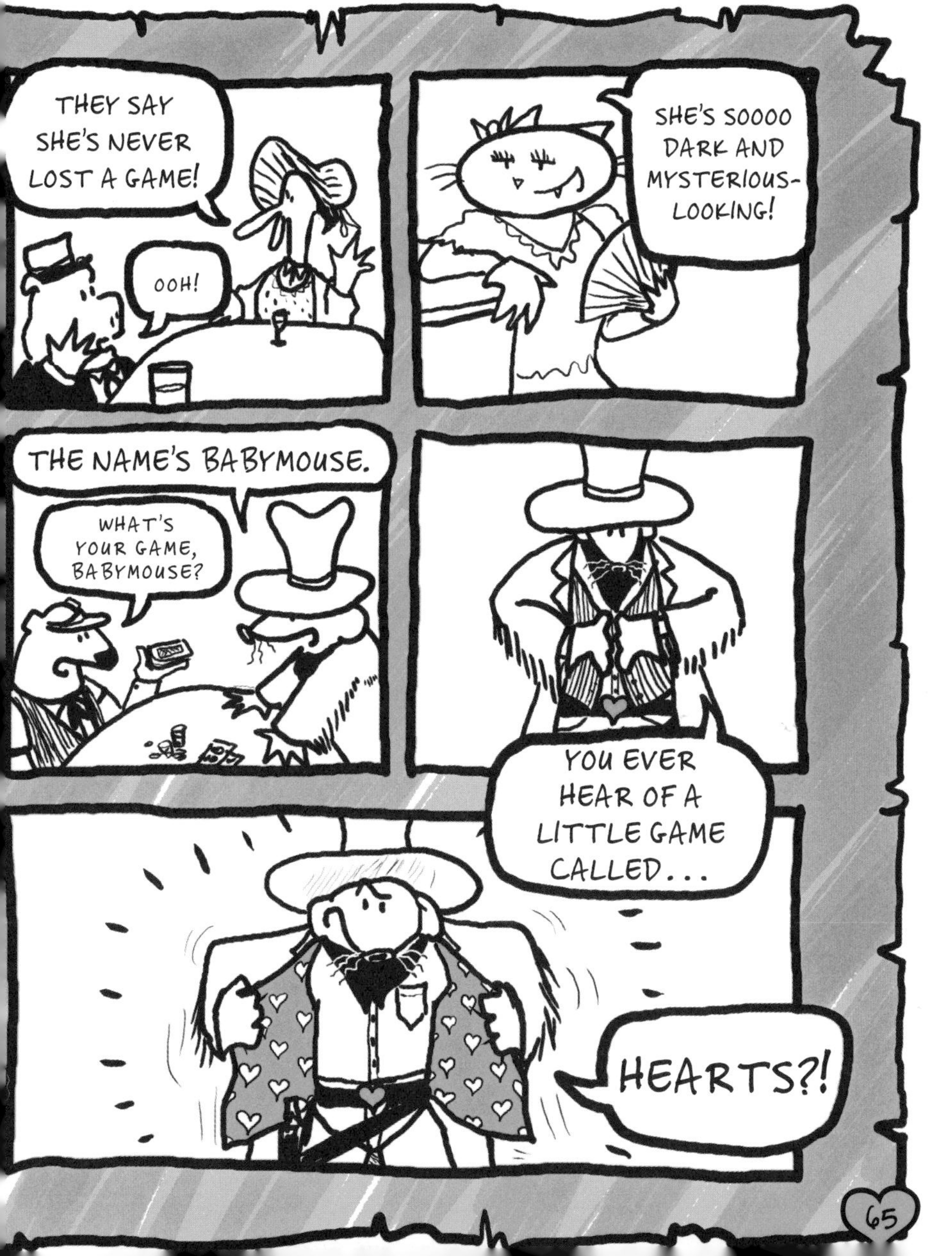

THEY SAY SHE'S NEVER LOST A GAME!
OOH!
SHE'S SOOOO DARK AND MYSTERIOUS-LOOKING!
THE NAME'S BABYMOUSE.
WHAT'S YOUR GAME, BABYMOUSE?
YOU EVER HEAR OF A LITTLE GAME CALLED...
HEARTS?!

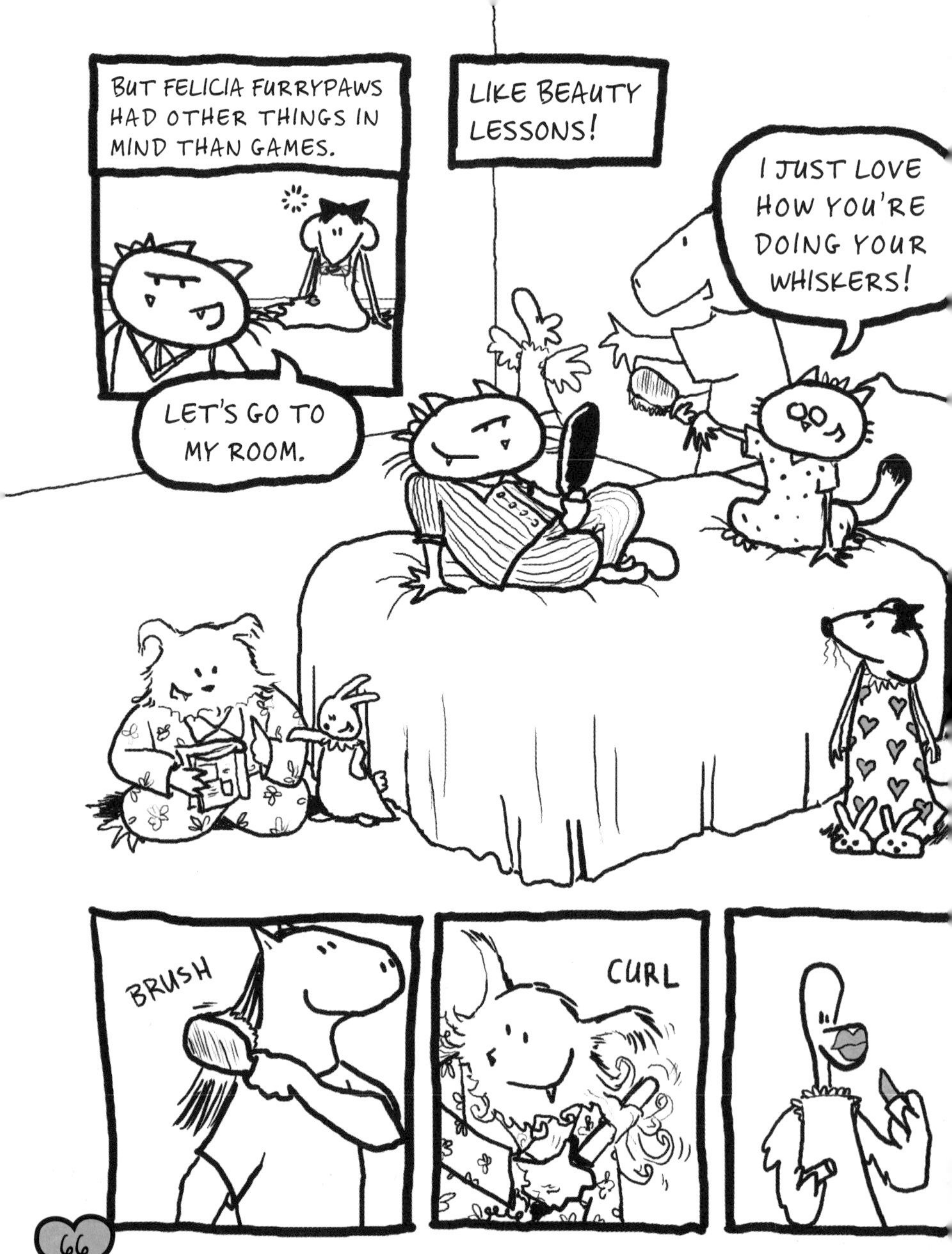
BUT FELICIA FURRYPAWS HAD OTHER THINGS IN MIND THAN GAMES.
LIKE BEAUTY LESSONS!
LET'S GO TO MY ROOM.
I JUST LOVE HOW YOU'RE DOING YOUR WHISKERS!
BRUSH
CURL

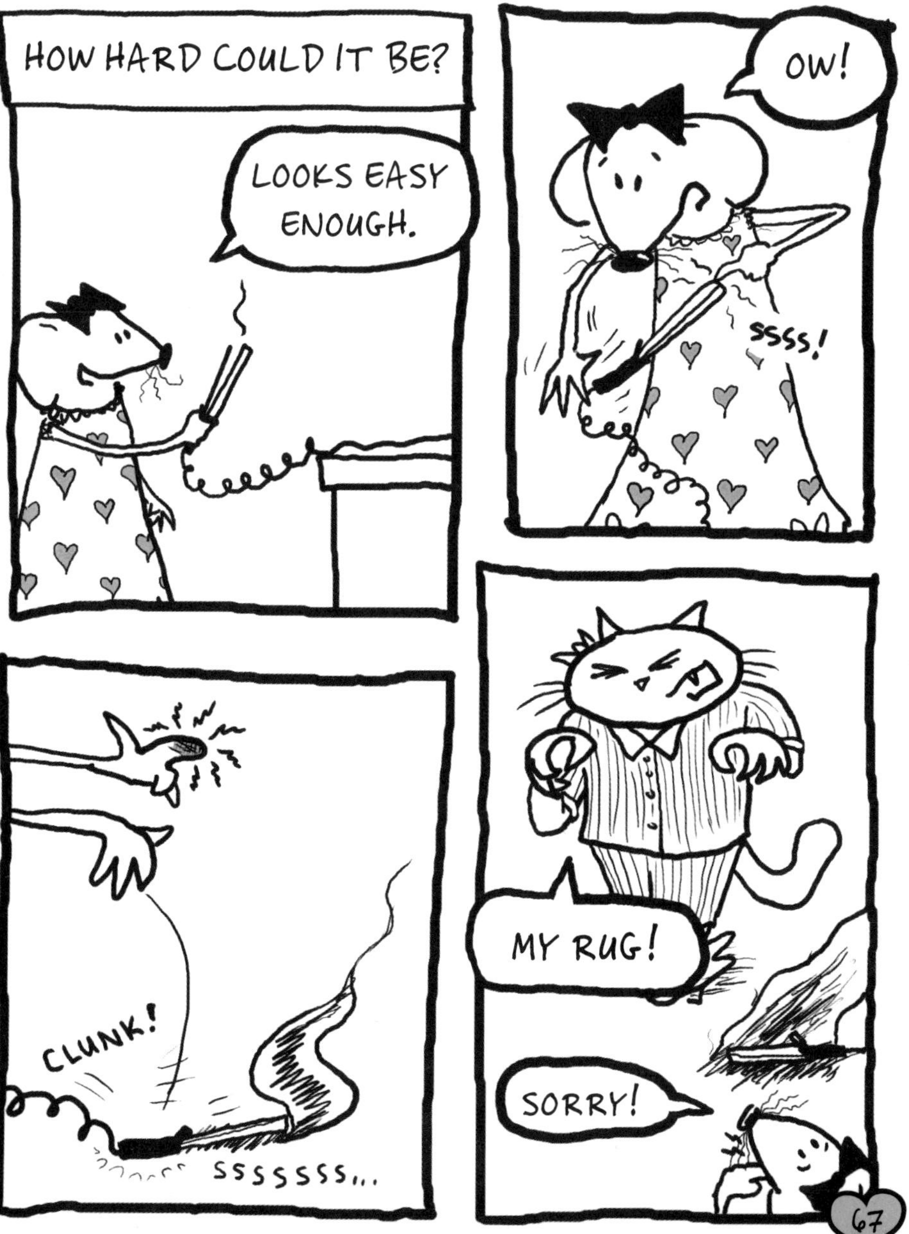
HOW HARD COULD IT BE?
LOOKS EASY ENOUGH.
OW!
SSSS!
CLUNK!
SSSSSSS...
MY RUG!
SORRY!

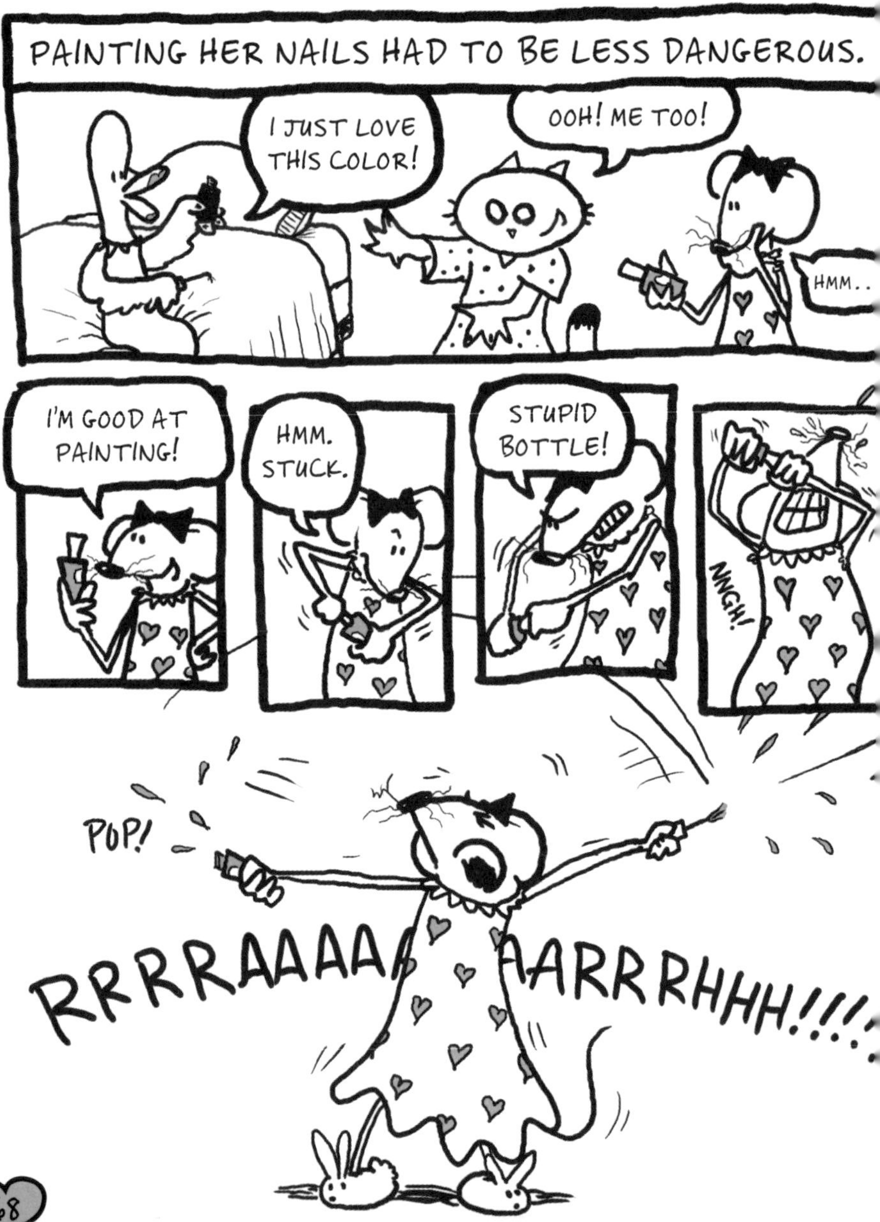
PAINTING HER NAILS HAD TO BE LESS DANGEROUS.
I JUST LOVE THIS COLOR!
OOH! ME TOO!
HMM...
I'M GOOD AT PAINTING!
HMM. STUCK.
STUPID BOTTLE!
NNGH!
POP!
RRRRAAAAAAARRRRHHH!!!!

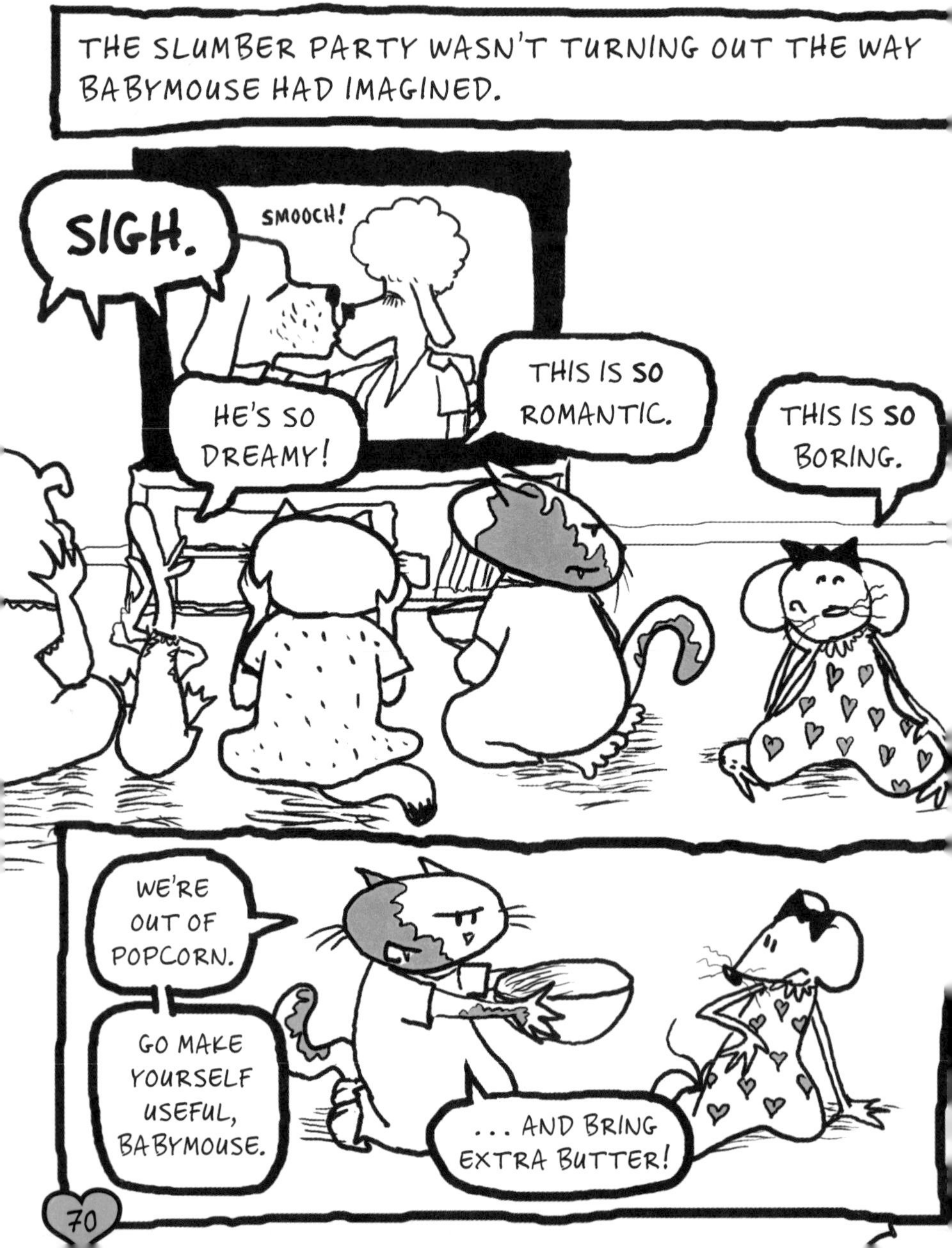
THE SLUMBER PARTY WASN'T TURNING OUT THE WAY BABYMOUSE HAD IMAGINED.
SIGH.
SMOOCH!
HE'S SO DREAMY!
THIS IS SO ROMANTIC.
THIS IS SO BORING.
WE'RE OUT OF POPCORN.
GO MAKE YOURSELF USEFUL, BABYMOUSE.
... AND BRING EXTRA BUTTER!

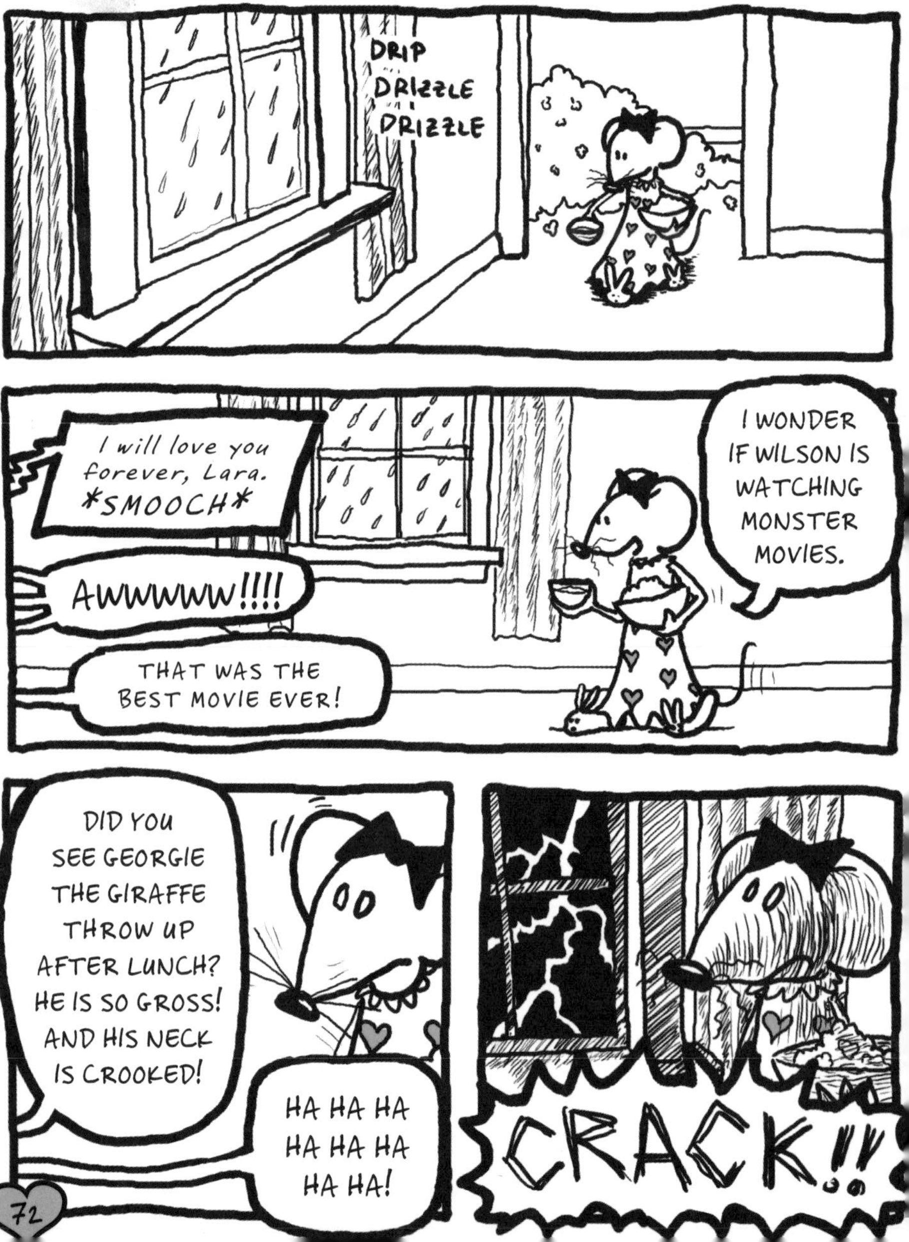
DRIP
DRIZZLE
DRIZZLE
I will love you forever, Lara. *SMOOCH*
AWWWWW!!!!
THAT WAS THE BEST MOVIE EVER!
I WONDER IF WILSON IS WATCHING MONSTER MOVIES.
DID YOU SEE GEORGIE THE GIRAFFE THROW UP AFTER LUNCH? HE IS SO GROSS! AND HIS NECK IS CROOKED!
HA HA HA HA HA HA HA HA!
CRACK!!!

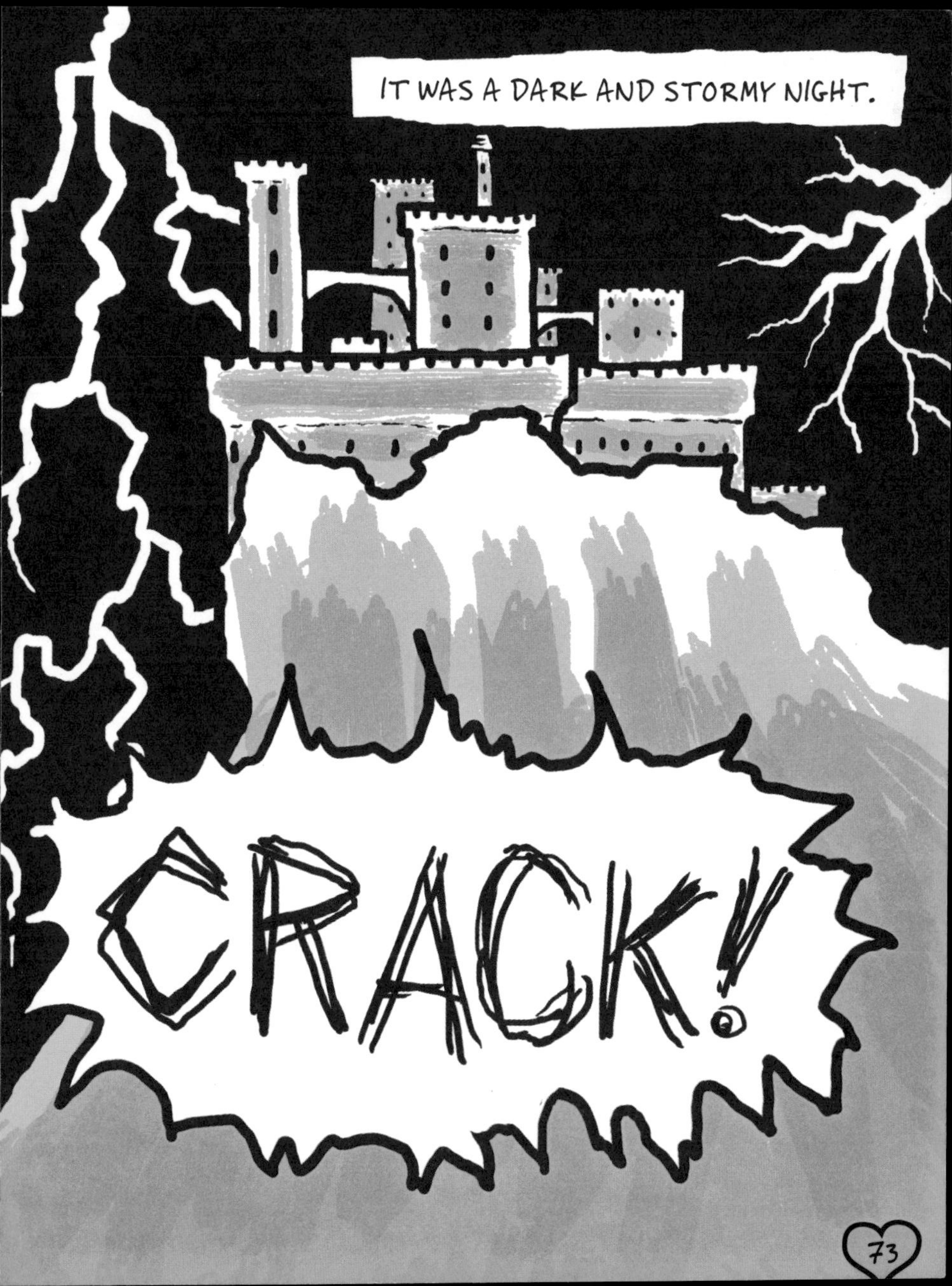
IT WAS A DARK AND STORMY NIGHT.
CRACK!

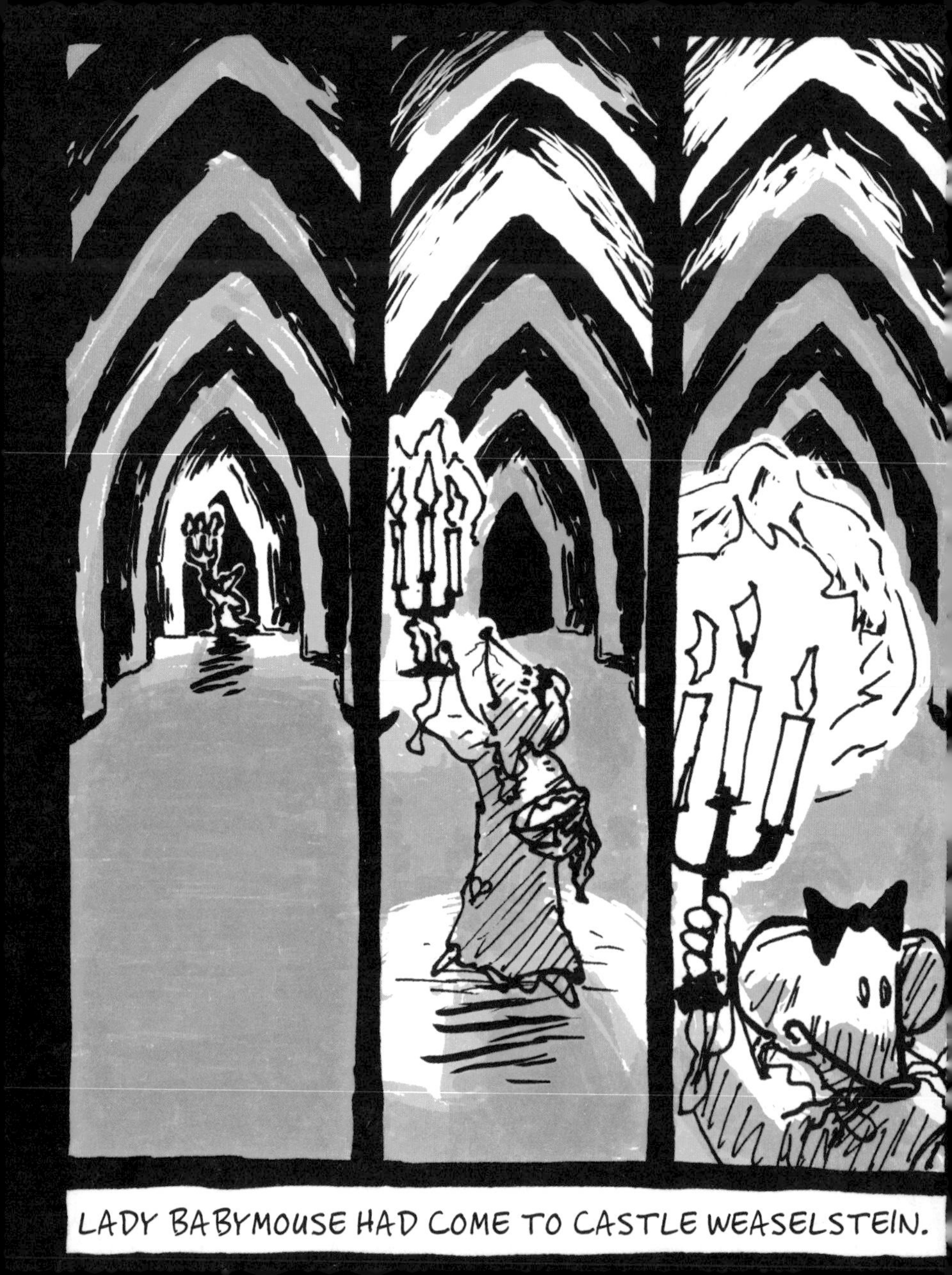
LADY BABYMOUSE HAD COME TO CASTLE WEASELSTEIN.

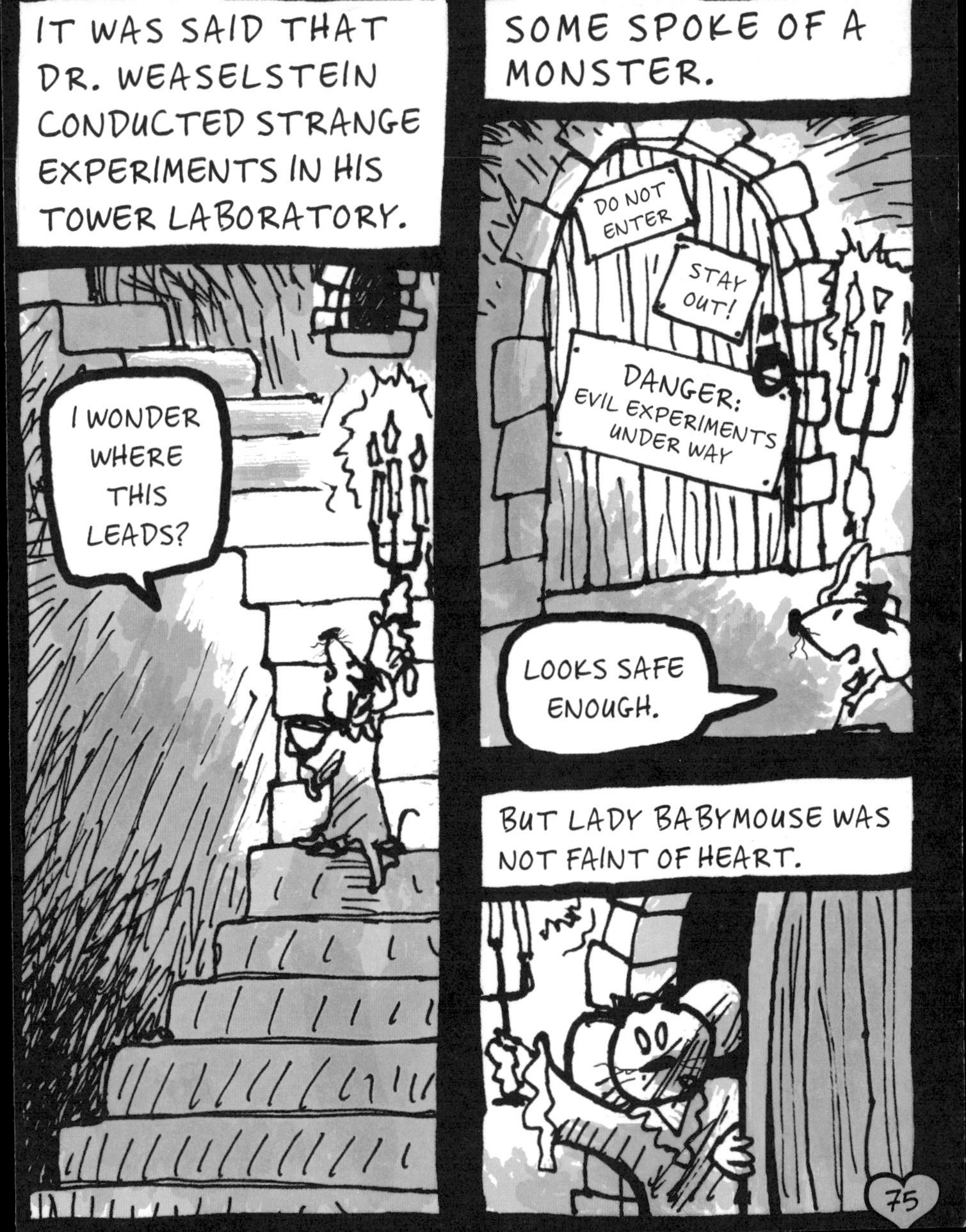
IT WAS SAID THAT DR. WEASELSTEIN CONDUCTED STRANGE EXPERIMENTS IN HIS TOWER LABORATORY.
I WONDER WHERE THIS LEADS?
SOME SPOKE OF A MONSTER.
DO NOT ENTER
STAY OUT!
DANGER: EVIL EXPERIMENTS UNDER WAY
LOOKS SAFE ENOUGH.
BUT LADY BABYMOUSE WAS NOT FAINT OF HEART.

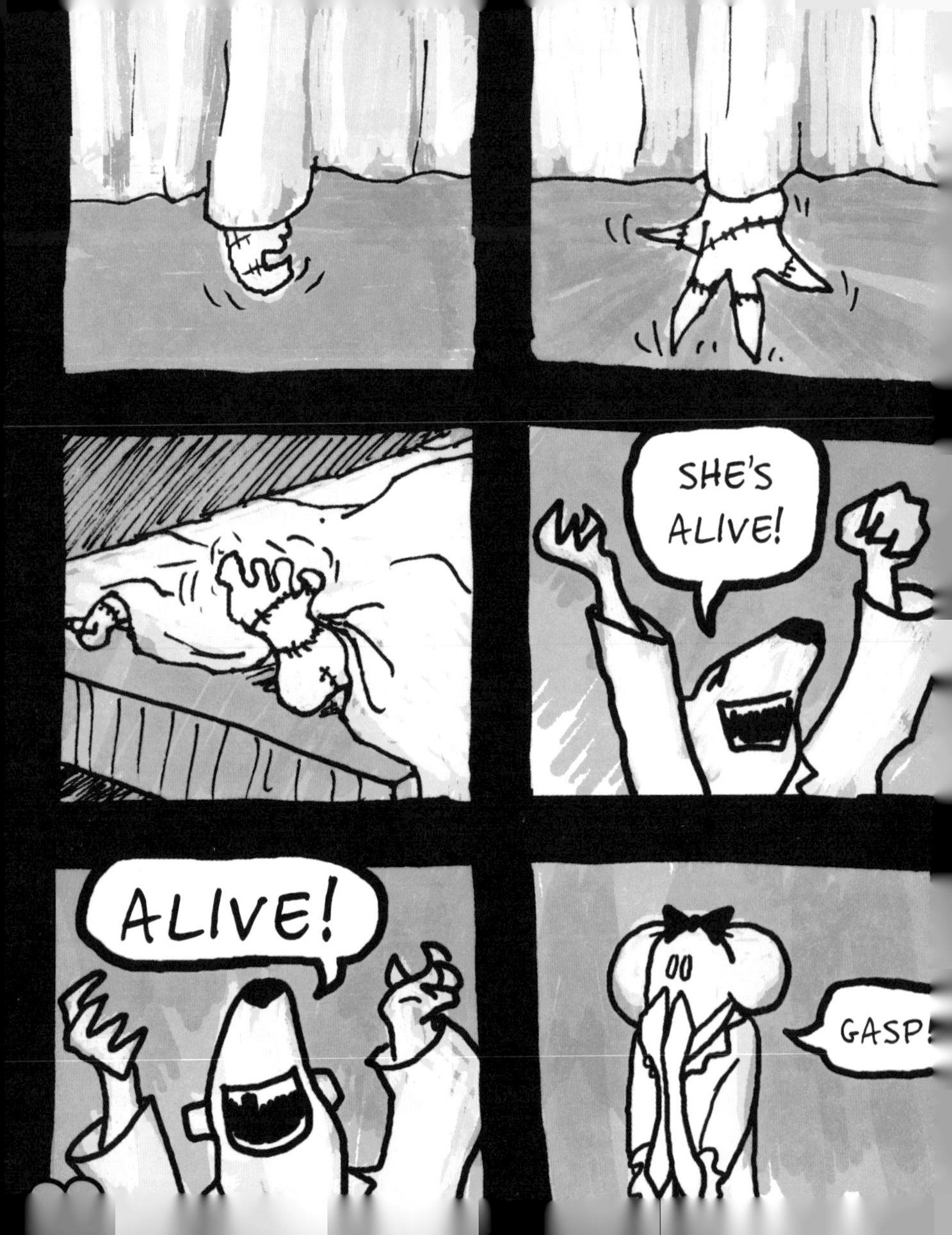
SHE'S ALIVE!
ALIVE!
GASP!

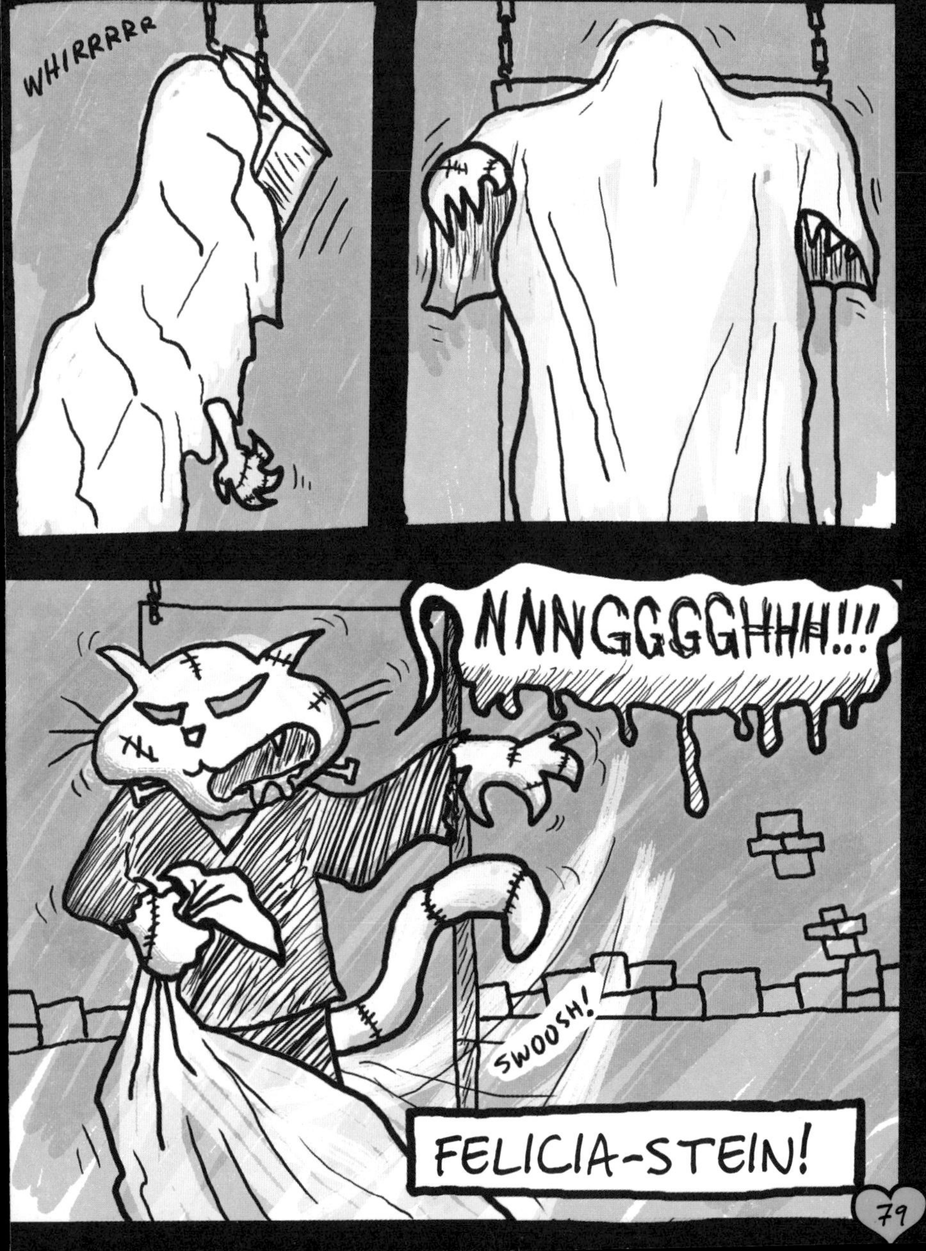
WHIRRRRR
NNNGGGGHHH!!!
SWOOSH!
FELICIA-STEIN!

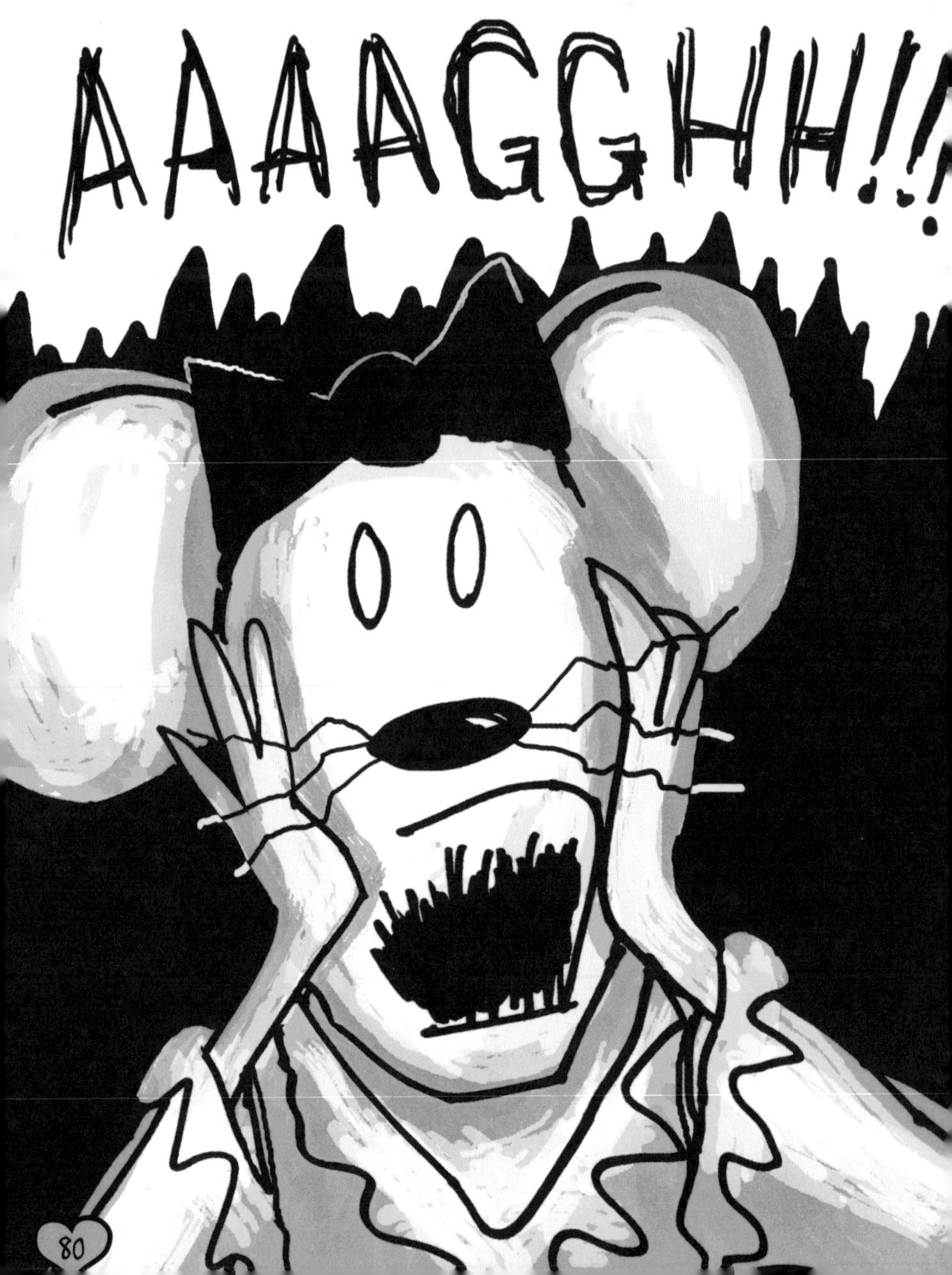
AAAAGGHH!!

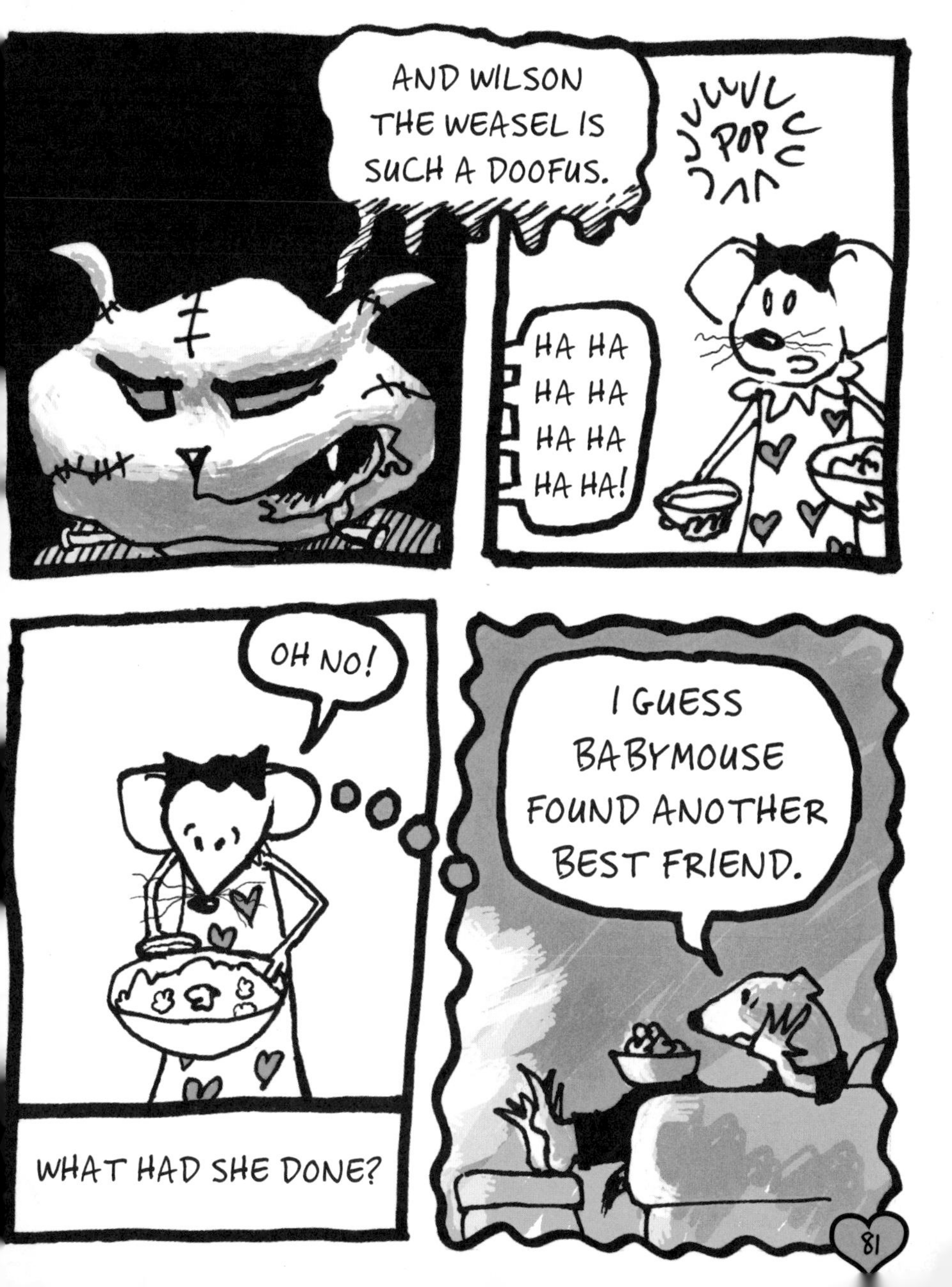
AND WILSON THE WEASEL IS SUCH A DOOFUS.
POP
HA HA HA HA HA HA HA HA!
OH NO!
I GUESS BABYMOUSE FOUND ANOTHER BEST FRIEND.
WHAT HAD SHE DONE?

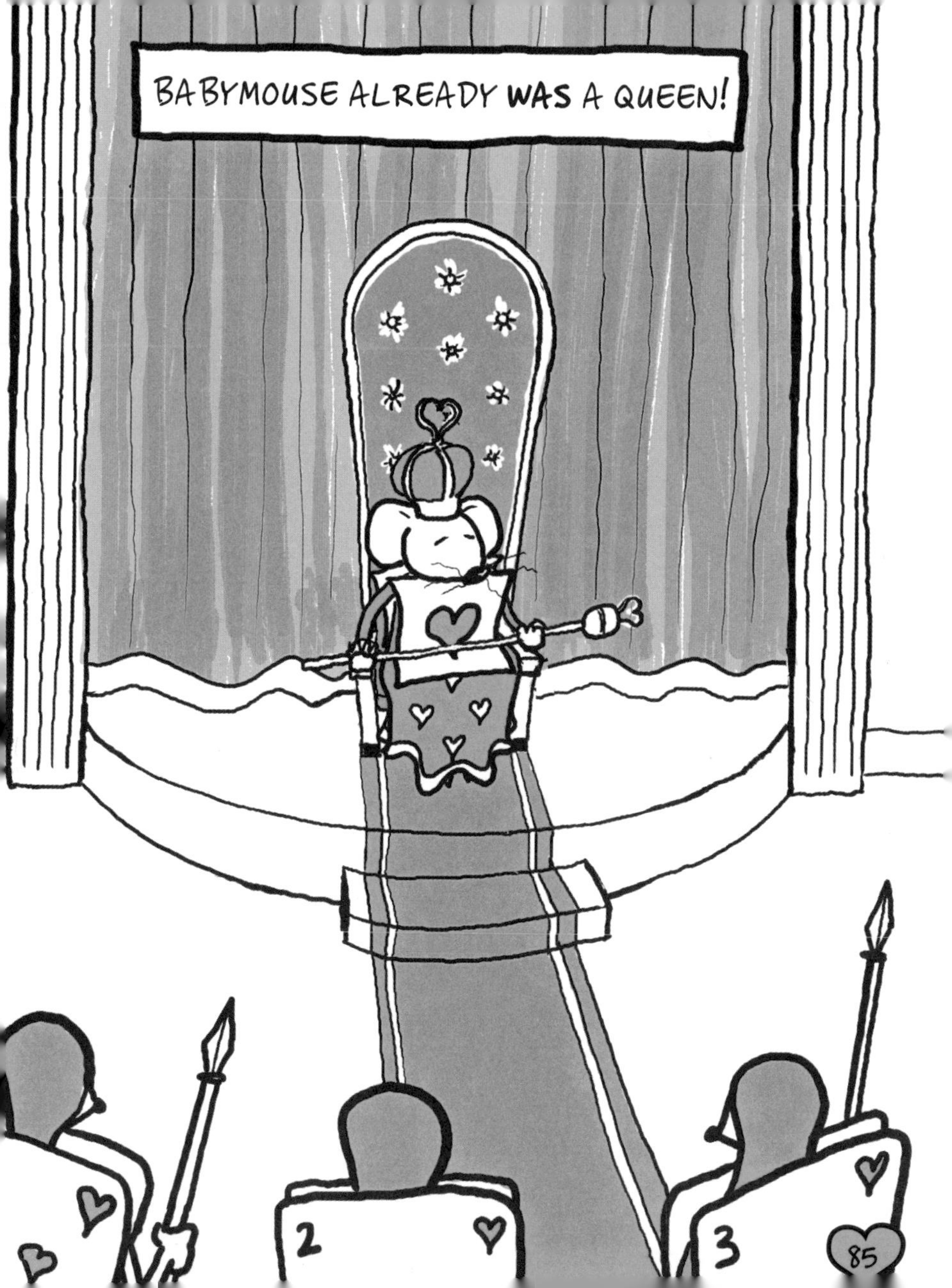
BABYMOUSE ALREADY WAS A QUEEN!
2
3

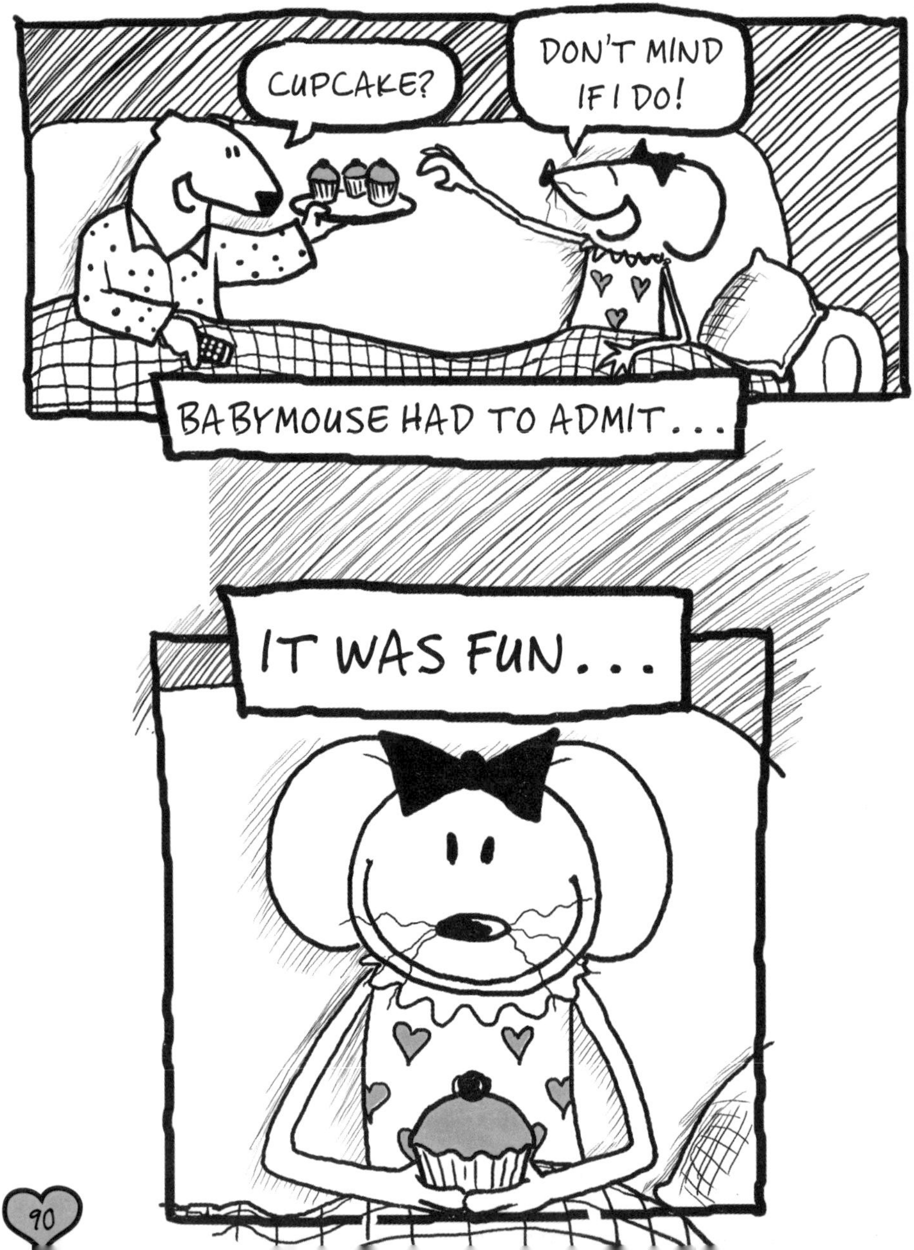
CUPCAKE?
DON'T MIND IF I DO!
BABYMOUSE HAD TO ADMIT...
IT WAS FUN...

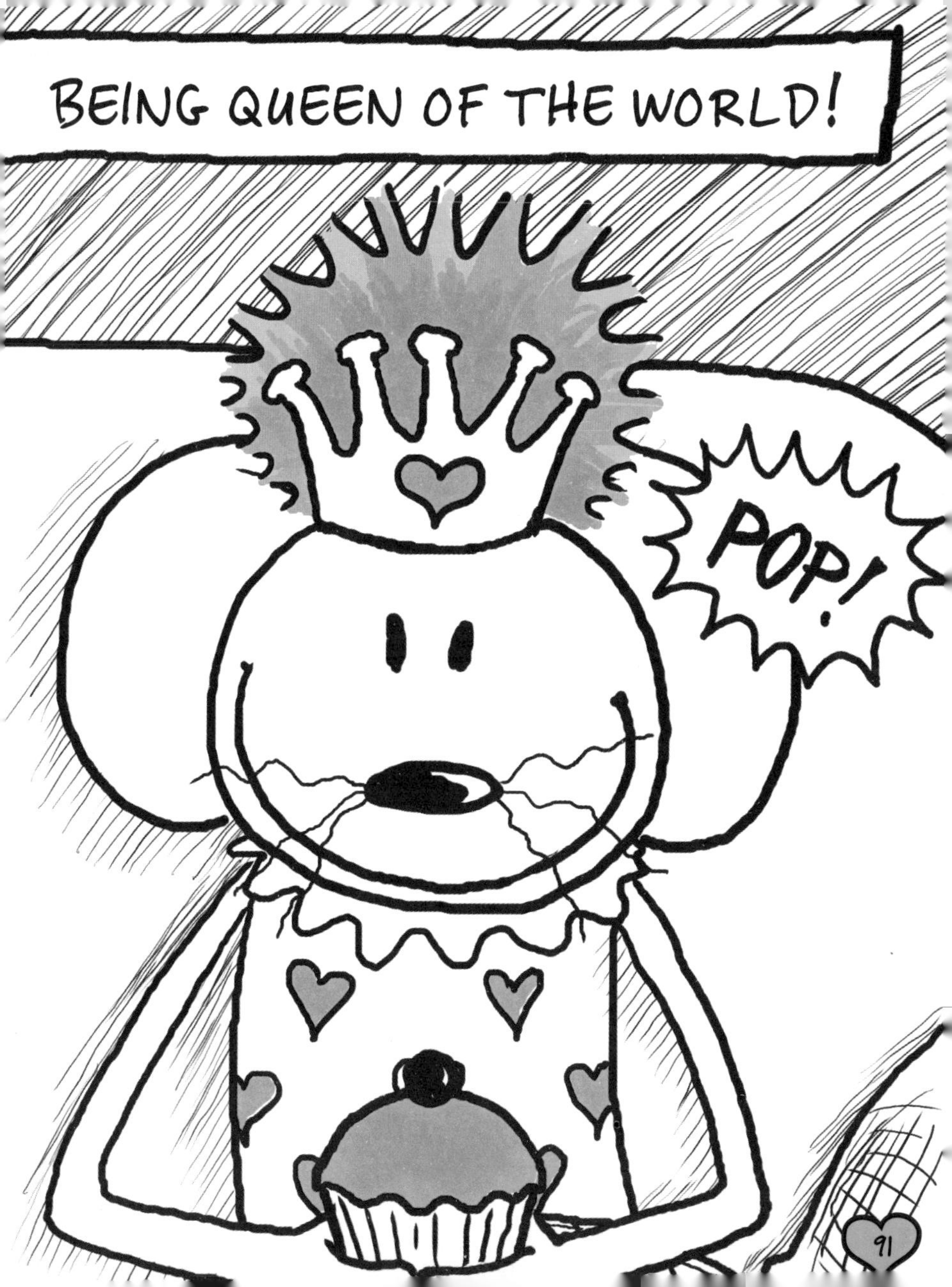
BEING QUEEN OF THE WORLD!
POP!

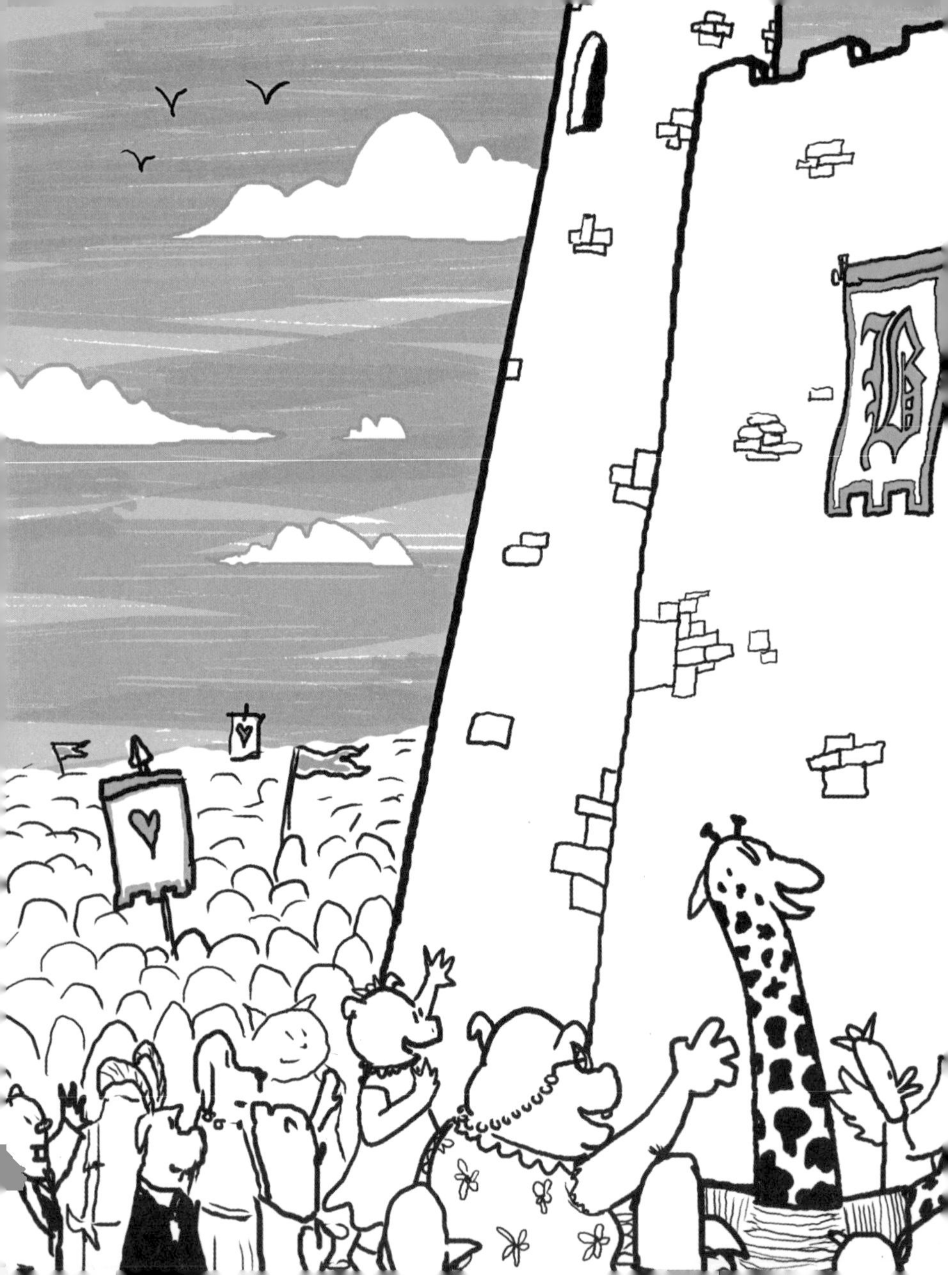
B

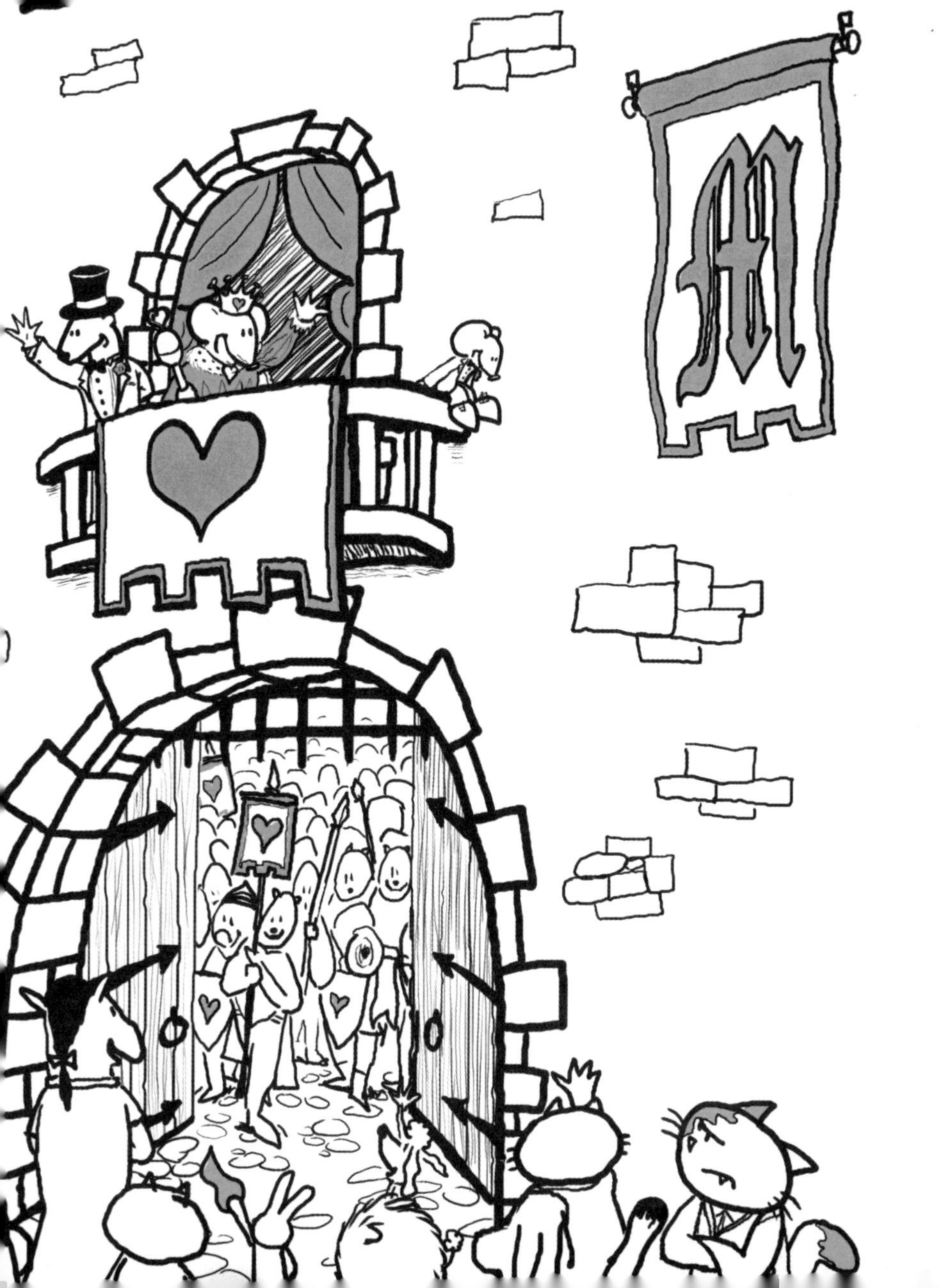
M

BABYMOUSE BONUS!

•LEARN HOW TO DRAW BABYMOUSE•

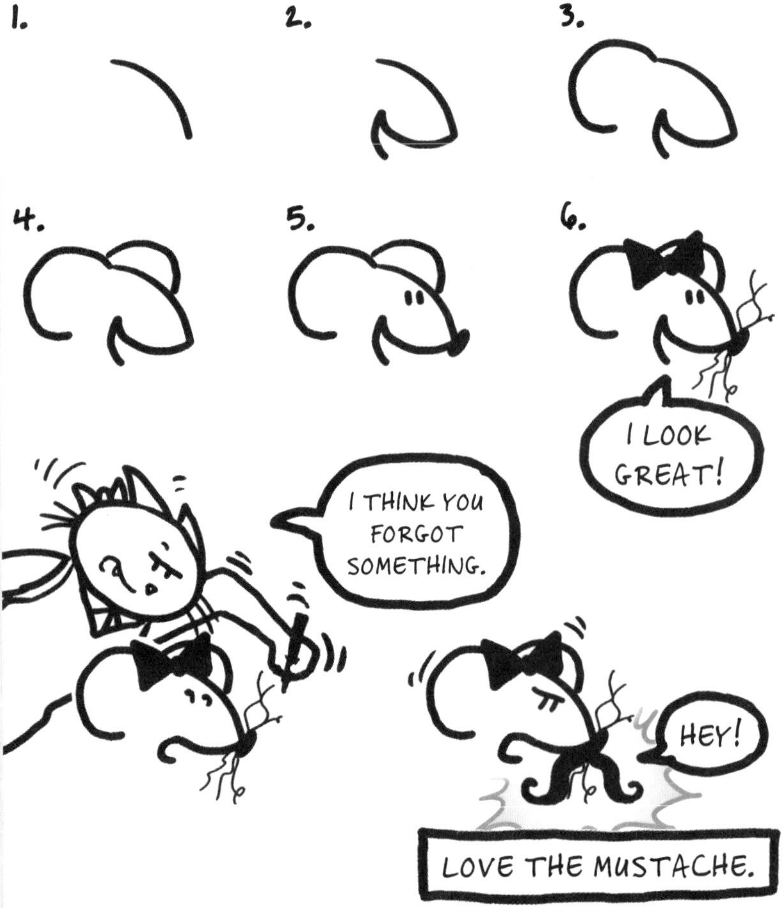
1.
2.
3.
4.
5.
6.
I LOOK GREAT!
I THINK YOU FORGOT SOMETHING.
HEY!
LOVE THE MUSTACHE.

BABYMOUSE BONUS!

•FILL IT IN AND MAKE YOUR OWN COMIC•

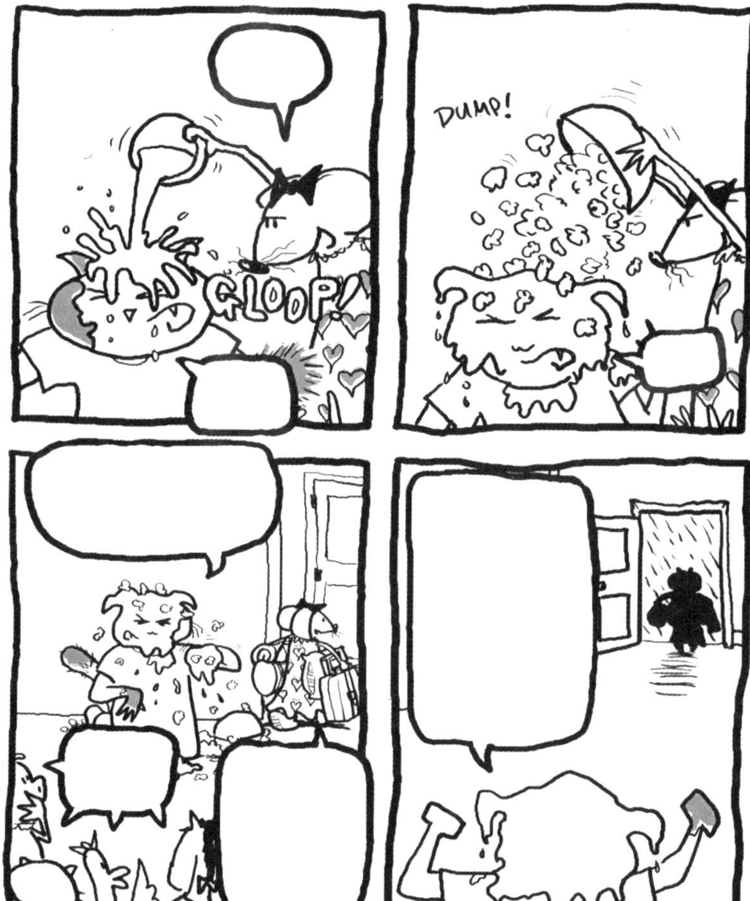
GLOOP!
DUMP!

BABYMOUSE BONUS!

•TIPS ON BEING QUEEN OF THE WORLD•

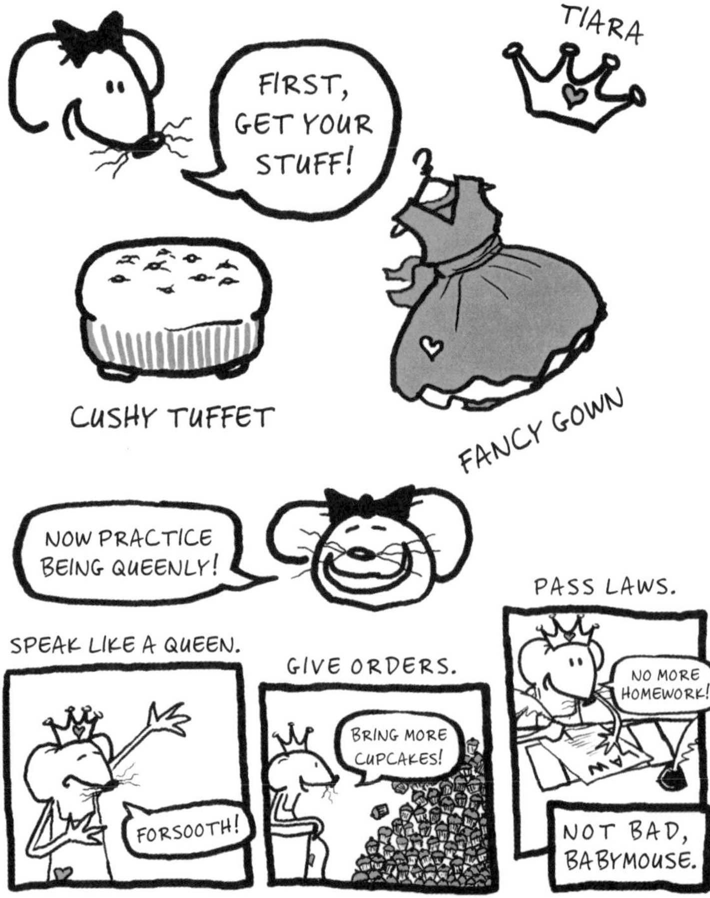

FIRST, GET YOUR STUFF!
TIARA
CUSHY TUFFET
FANCY GOWN
NOW PRACTICE BEING QUEENLY!
SPEAK LIKE A QUEEN.
FORSOOTH!
GIVE ORDERS.
BRING MORE CUPCAKES!
PASS LAWS.
NO MORE HOMEWORK!
LAW
NOT BAD, BABYMOUSE.